BY JAKOV LIND   *Soul of Wood*

Landscape in Concrete

Ergo

ERGO

JAKOV LIND

translated from

RANDOM

RGO

e German by RALPH MANHEIM

OUSE, New York

FIRST AMERICAN EDITION

Library of Congress Catalog Card Number: 67–22649

© Copyright, 1967, by Random House, Inc. and Methuen & Co. Ltd.
All rights reserved under International and Pan American Copyright Con-
ventions. Published in New York by Random House, Inc., and simul-
taneously in Toronto, Canada, by Random House of Canada Limited.
Originally published in German as "Eine bessere Welt" © 1966, by
Verlag Klaus Wagenbach, Berlin. Manufactured in the United States of
America by American Book–Stratford Press, Inc., New York.

Designed by KENNETH MIYAMOTO

For Anne and Maxwell Geismar

ERGO

ERGO: where the meadow narrows and the river makes a bend there is a sunken ship made of old beams and corrugated iron, stone flags and doors that don't close properly, a jerry-built structure with rough wooden boards instead of windows that calls itself Custom House No. 8. Here at the end of a footpath it has lain rotting away for the last eighty or a hundred years. No one pays attention to it, because if you notice it from the bridge it looks like a piece of driftwood, but you don't notice it and no one has ever found out who if anybody lives there.

The pink storks and the white herons are painting geometry in the pale grayness over the river, over a hungry tug. A steamboat making its getaway after conquering the city retreats downstream, leaving heat and sweat behind it on the meadows and on the bald skull of Aslan Schepretz, who is jiggling up and down in front of a small mirror, asking himself who am I and where am I, appeased only when he recognizes his little brown teeth. The others are still asleep.

To one side, his hand between his legs, lies Leo Schön-Waldhaus, short, dark and bearded, wheezing out the end of a deep sleep through his big nose, and down below in the storeroom, protruding from the white mountain of paper, a brown vestige of Roman Wacholder, who is lying fully dressed on his belly, weeping and still asleep.

How anybody can sleep in such a place of his own free will is more than Aslan can understand. He stands up and looks down, but he doesn't think anything until Wacholder suddenly shouts: I am the animal. That frightens Aslan, and he runs into his room. I am the animal has made Leo jump out of bed. With his right hand Leo rubs the sleep from his eyes, with his left he holds his underdrawers. He then blows his nose between thumb and forefinger and finally finds words: Your goddamned leprosy, you need a woman, it's unhealthy always lying in that paper—shut up, it's Sunday. Wacholder has no words. He sees his friends up top (Aslan has ventured out again) and sighs. There they are, talking about me, he wants to cry out but can't.

Guilt was identical with Wacholder, there was nothing to amputate. I stabbed her—yes, I stabbed her from the inside—he confessed after May 15, 1959, after his lawyer had certified that the affair had come under the statute of limitations. The thing was big and looked dangerous but didn't even weigh five pounds, and he didn't, as people claimed, carry it in a shopping bag that he somehow tied on to himself with string. It was impressive, but it wasn't a butcher shop or a chimney; it was neither industry nor public welfare, but history, the history of crime, if you will. It actually grew, not much, but even a little was too much, and put on weight with the improved food situation of the first postwar years, and one would almost have said that it couldn't be effaced unless you effaced Wacholder himself, but where was there a judge who would sign such a sentence nowadays? A man is identical with his cock. A lawyer has to know such things, and the lawyer also predicted that justice would surely prevail. Justice had prevailed, inspired by Leo, who had written *The Placental Theory of Existence*—he ought to have written something about the metaphysics of my cock, but Leo was already writing and Aslan was writing too. Aslan was writing a novel that was to be entitled *The Better World*. The nonwriting Wacholder was alone with his religion and bad dreams.

Slowly and heavily, a hippopotamus rising from the Nile, he rose from the paper mountain, beat the nightmare of virginal lewdness out of his clothes and stood there, a squat man of sixty with short gray hair and swollen lips, crossing his hands over his forehead, and looked around him darkly. Have you been watching me again while I was asleep? Have you been spying on me, you scum? You're living by my sufferance, remember that. Tomorrow it will be all up with you. I'll throw you both out. Both of you. What time is it?

5

Nine o'clock, Father. Aslan called him Father because of the difference in their ages and in token of devotion and gratitude. Nine o'clock, eh? Wacholder was now able to shout, so he shouted.

Yes, nine o'clock, Father.

What about my tea?

Leo jumped out of bed again (has he gone plumb crazy?) and picked at his molar with satisfaction as Aslan obediently brought down his own tea. Aslan can do what he likes, I'm here to work.

Wacholder warmed his hands on the lukewarm tea. They've been here again, Aslan, the big black ones, do you hear. They've visited me again, Aslan, as big as gothic letters, up and down the wall of my heart, Aslan, up and down, and the Latin letters too, as green and thick as creepers. A whole bellyful, Aslan, it turned my stomach, Aslan. And then the rats, as big as big steamships, back and forth, back and forth. What do you think, Aslan, should I call the doctor?

Call the doctor, Father.

No, I won't call the doctor. I've changed my mind. Let them crawl, let them bob up and down, let them gnaw and creep and root about. Let them hollow me out. Man is a pipe.

Yes, Father.

Man is a connecting pipe between feed trough and garbage pail. Here's the trough and here's the pail, and across here is man and they send things through him. A hose. You see what I mean?

Yes, Father.

Do I get Würz or don't I?

Not for the present, Father.

He's half my mutilated soul, do you understand that at least?

There's something between the two of you. Something. Something that cuts across the river and through all the walls. An umbilical cord.

That's it, Aslan. An umbilical cord.

You're twins. Still unborn.

That's it, my dear poet.

Nibbling in your sleep at the placenta of this world.

That's right, Aslan, that's right.

Floating in the dark, amniotic fluid . . .

Yes, Aslan, we're both floating. I in my bleached wood fibers, in my glue, breathless, airless, and he over there on the other side in his madness. Have you drafted the letter?

Here it is, Father. The seventy-fourth.

Let's see.

Wacholder stared at a large sheet of paper crowded with writing and turned it in all directions. My eyes hurt. Read it to me.

Aslan read: Now, Würz, you've got to go. And quick. The house is on fire. Your face is black with smoke and soot. Get down to the river. You're on fire. Into the sand with you. Put yourself out. Make it fast. Drop your brushes. Run. The beams are falling. Hurry. The house-cleaning can wait. Out with you. The fire is consuming you. You're half charred. You eggshell. You sheet of wrapping paper. You tree-stump goblin. You tin can. Run for your life. I'll put you out in Greenland. Don't be afraid.

Seventeen years is enough. Hurry up. Yours, Wacholder.

Read it again.

Aslan read the letter a second time. Wacholder scratched his temples, pondered. Okay. He was satisfied.

He's my friend, Aslan. Wacholder spoke sadly, with a hoarse faraway voice. My friend, he croaked, I'm loyal to him. Always will be.

That's right, Wacholder.

No Wacholder is going to leave his best friend to his fate. Not me. Never. He's locked himself up—he's going to be set free. What's inside's got to come out. Can't stay in forever. Because life too is a pipe, Aslan, especially human life. It flows and flows, but it can also get clogged. Würz is clogged up, I mean he's clogged up his life. That's not what I wanted, but I couldn't prevent it. He didn't deserve it. No one's to blame. The war. What can you do?

No one's to blame, Wacholder, you're right.

No, no one's to blame. I said it then and I say it now: people who deserve a Hitler get a Hitler, and people who don't deserve a Hitler don't get a Hitler. Hitler can't help it.

No, Father.

Nobody knows why everything around here is so placental, but everybody realizes that it's normal, because here everything is normal. This is my town.

A town made of Liptauer cream cheese, Lippizaner horses and Lilliputians of roast chicken, bauernschmaus, liver dumplings and liver sausage, a rhyme, a phrase, a proverb and perhaps not even that but only a waistline, a shoe size, a collar size, a hat size and perhaps not even that but only the family vault of Maria Theresa and Franz Josef and the children Kalifati, Rübezahl, Krampus, and Nikolo Christkindl and Andreas Hofer, who died of scarlet fever, whooping cough, measles, chicken pox and Basedow's disease.

In the municipal hospital, where the saviour was born into the world, the saviour of the Kahlenberg, who went upstream to Kriau to free Richard Lowenherz from Mauthausen, but now he too is dead and buried at the central cemetery, to sleep forever side by side with Lueger and Seitz Kaltenbrunner and Mozart. There he lies with Dollfuss and Fey and Robert Stricker of the Zionist league, and Prince Eugene, who freed Vienna from the Turks, and the heroes of the Karlmarxhof and the heroes of the Heimwehr, and nobody knows how there can conceivably be such a city.

Which calls itself the teat of the occident and has suckled nothing but madness.

2 The twenty-four houses came to an end at a twenty-foot wall. At the window of soundproof and bulletproof glass stood Würz, with his hands behind his back, staring at his landscape. A forgotten street in a neighborhood inhabited only by pensioned couples and lonely old women, many of them invalids. Everything looked normal.

He didn't see it at first, then he couldn't take his eyes off it. There it sat. The Devil itself only blacker. The cat from No. 12, the only one still living in the street, was the shadow in his eyes, the lead in his bones that prevented him from going out, and the dirt in his pores that couldn't be removed, that he had been trying for seventeen years to remove. Washing and licking herself, and looking up at the same time. He could feel the damp pinkness, the cat spittle in his stomach. With the same tongue she licked away his face, his body, his whole existence. Würz made faces, and when that didn't help he spat at the windowpane and wiped it off immediately. Burning it in effigy twenty times didn't do any good, neither did magic spells, I've got to kill her, I've got to, or she'll eat me. Here lies Ossias Würz, devoured by a cat. I've got to do something before it's too late. But he did nothing. This cat was part of a world he had left seventeen years before. That world he called the Outside.

Outside, the air is gray and full of germs.

Outside, human existence is impossible. Smoke and gases and used-up oxygen from millions of lungs, the moist slime of rain, the slimy seed of snow. At the mercy of the foul-smelling wind, threatened by shaky scaffoldings that could crush you at any moment. And the dirt that covers it all. Every atom out there contains the contigent, the morose, the so-called eternal-perishable. And all that nature romanticism, that natural obscenity. The freedom of chaos is nature in its original state, the freedom of chaos is decay and death. The jungle we have to clear away is freedom.

A pair of aged hands transformed the blackness by enchantment into two empty milk bottles.

Würz turned away from the window to devote himself to the essential.

Fire didn't worry him. Wacholder had used more effective threats. Cats, rats, ants, dynamite, floods. What worried him wasn't the substance or the curses. What bothered him was that people didn't take him and his work seriously. Ossias Würz was frantically busy making preparations for his seventeenth wedding anniversary. And now comes this letter, the seventy-fourth, and the preparations have to be postponed. As usual, he first put Wacholder's letter in an envelope. So as not to forget it, he wrote Wacholder's address on the outside (Alsterhof, City) and affixed a stamp. Only then did he start working on the answer.

Good Lord, Wacholder, what's got into you again, what are you driving at with your fire? I'm burning with eagerness to do my work, and you want to smoke me out of here. How often must I tell you that I want to be left in peace? I need peace to do my peaceful work. I wish to build, not to sit around, to preserve, not to destroy. I am a man of progress, a man of the future, I have values, yes, values. I am the future. The future is I. Don't you see that? Me a sheet of wrapping paper, an eggshell, an empty tin can? And where do you get the tree-stump goblin? I'm

11

telling you for the last time: my home is not a cave. This is no womb, it doesn't smell of sweat and blood, of milk and urine, of afterbirth and yesterday. Don't make me think of those things, I'm always thinking of them. And when I think of them, I feel as I did then. It was an uninterrupted movement of the lips, eating deeper and deeper into the flesh. It was hunger, lust. If you remember, stop remembering. Those were the lip-smacking years, but we didn't get fat. Not I. Did you? It took me a long time, but now I know. It's no good chasing after your daily bread, don't move from your four walls. Exertion is a waste of energy. I have all nature delivered to my back door. Here in my home it's chopped small and grated fine, crushed and salted, boiled and eaten. I've got my domestic animals in jars and bottles. That's the way to do it. And the beauties of nature aren't lacking either. I have butterflies in tissue paper, a marten and a fox on top of the cupboard, two elks, a roe and a bear on the wall. A swallow and a sea gull under glass. And it's all fresh and clean. Here I can breathe. I don't need your Greenland or your river, and I can do without your café. What would I do in your café? What have you to offer me? A noise that's always in my ears? Faces that smack their lips and talk and stare at me, that I see the whole time as it is? What have you got out there that I haven't got in here? Neatness and order are freedom, that's why I stay here.

Satisfied with his letter, he folded it into the envelope and lay down in order to get ahead with his preparations. At last he'd told him, that's what he'd always wanted to say. He sends me fire, I send him distilled water to wash

his eyes with so at last he'll see. He's provocative, I'm
indulgent. Würz is a mighty fortress that will soon be
celebrating the seventeenth anniversary of its founding.
Seventeen years of conscientious work and order. Seventeen years of marriage. It began eighteen years ago. Eighteen years ago I saw her for the first time. Where was it?
The circumstances? It was a Sunday, a Sunday afternoon
in the summer. I was wearing a uniform under my raincoat. Still working for the gas company. Did you call for a
gas man? This is Sunday. I'm doing overtime. Come in.
Would you like to see my clock? As long as I'm here, yes,
do let me see your clock. Here it is. It counts too fast. It's
too expensive. Your clock doesn't run as it should, am I
right? Yes, it runs wrong. May I feel it for a moment, just
to test it? Yes, you're right. A fast clock, a clock that's in a
hurry. My name is Rita Hauch. Mrs. Rita Hauch, your
clock doesn't count as it should. I'll put in a report. You
really will? Immediately, without delay, tomorrow morning to be exact. There's something wrong in your place.
Something is out of order, but without the approval of my
office, which of course I shall obtain immediately, I'm
sorry, besides, on Sunday, I have no tools, it's not custom-
ary. Otherwise, I assure you, there's nothing I'd rather.
Oh, you are a nice man. Ossias Würz is the name. Oh,
dear Mr. Ossias Würz, how can I thank you? Don't thank
me. Since it's Sunday and I have cake on Sunday, baked
with your company's gas. No thank you, I'm on duty. Oh
please, Mr. Würz, just a little piece. All right, half a
piece, so to speak, because I'm only half on duty. A Sunday, Mrs. Hauch, doesn't encourage one to feel the full

weight of duty. I baked it myself, with your gas, with your own gas, Mr. Würz. Splendid, Mrs. Hauch, your cake is excellent, an excellent poppy-seed cake. Oh, how you talk, I must thank you for the compliment. I must thank you. No, I you. No, I you. How sweetly she laughs, how she crinkles up her little nose, and how coyly she hides her little teeth. A sweet little kitten. What pretty little ears and so downy. And now with her right paw she takes fourteen crumbs and kneads them between thumb and forefinger and pops them whoosh into her mouth. She's a clean little animal. Are you alone, Mr. Würz? His heart beats, the little animal can speak. On Sunday, I always go out alone, but even on other days I'm often alone. I don't care for just any company. Are you alone, Mrs. Hauch? I'm never alone, I have two children, Mr. Würz. Two boys. Arnulf and Arnold. No, I'm never alone. I don't know the meaning of solitude. Only loneliness.

Only loneliness, Mrs. Hauch? Draw the curtains. Undo a dress. Unlace heavy work shoes. Hang raincoat on a hook in the hall. Suit on hanger. Go to toilet. Wash hands. Rinse mouth. Remove and fold bedspread. Turn key in lock. Comb hair. All in less than eight minutes.

Big breasts, broad thighs. White. Hair, hair, hair all over. Black. A long neck. White with little brown spots in back. Black fuzz around the redness. A little mustache. Big dark eyes. The eyes of a pregnant cat. And black short fuzzy hair all over. A furry little woman you can't help loving. And so I loved her and still love her.

Everything is fine and dandy, and at the same time all wrong. The world stands on its head and looks strikingly normal. I have nothing to reproach myself with and never stop reproaching myself. I have nothing to be afraid of and I'm always afraid.

This state of affairs is named Würz.

3 *The Better World* he had dedicated to his childhood, named Wacholder. Five pages were finished, five pages in a blue envelope he kept out of sight in a drawer, a book or under the mattress. Five secret and private pages, so secret and private that he had long ago decided never to complete the book. Never must this childhood fall into Wacholder's hands, for in these five pages everything was written in black and white, and Wacholder wouldn't hesitate, he would instantly strike him dead, for secret thoughts are punishable by death and these thoughts were especially secret, to be thought only behind a locked door barricaded with a chair; they were even more secret than the five pages, and for that reason he thought them only hesitantly. In a word, they were really secret thoughts. I am an idealist, the kind who really believes in man, who really believes in love, kindness and patience. Although nobody wants to believe it, I've never believed in anything else. I am a child, a child who is too awkward and childish for this life, a dependent child who believes in the love and kindness of grownups as if it were the most natural thing in the world, and it isn't but has always been for me and always will be, and that's exactly what's in it if you read it carefully, which is why no one must ever find out what's in it. No one but me.

Aslan took the pages and read them as silently and piously as a prayer at night, these secret pages written in a secret language designed to conceal his most secret thoughts.

A courtyard. Walls. Windows. A playground in the courtyard. A bench. There are five of us. She is little. In blue and white. Who said: Put it in? And who: The marble? We tried it. It didn't work. Somebody came and sent us away. A funeral procession in white. Soldiers are standing in the yard. Her father was a major in the Heimwehr. Cock feather and white gloves. Her mother in black. A white embroidered handkerchief. Is that a water lily opening above her closed hand? She smells the flower and does not cry. Not a single tear for her child. It wasn't the same child, or don't you cry when children die? They were both named Erika. In the coffin they carried me, not Erika. Erika can have my life. She can move into my home, where there is nothing. Only ugly pictures, bedbugs, salt, coal and flour. She can have it all, poor child who has a mother who doesn't cry. Mine would cry. And my father, who's never home, will get the white gloves and the cock feather on his cap. The first funeral was mine. I hid. Read Gorki. I loved Gorki. In the first place the name, in the second place his mustache, and then his stories. Everybody was poor and sad like us. He wrote our life. A sad, poor, depraved life, which in the end, even though no one expects it, becomes good, if not for the characters themselves, at least for their children or grandchildren. That was Gorki, who, behind his bushy eyebrows, which he held to his forehead like a hand, foresaw a better future. After Gorki came a stranger. Was he a barber or something of the kind? His mustache was small, he had curly hair, wore high boots and suspenders and always went into the kitchen for shaving water. In the kitchen he always had something to do, something always occurred to him to distract my mother. He robbed me of the time he took from my mother. With nonsense and stories about people and things I didn't understand. A stranger in the house. My father is gone. First you don't know. You doubt. And then you know. There's something between the two of them. My father will never find out. But I know, I can let the cat out of the bag. And I will. I'll tell him everything when he comes home. But he doesn't come. It doesn't even enter his head. He's gone forever. He'll never come back. And then he comes home after all. And leaves again right away. Brings a bear and leaves. I try to shout it after him, but he doesn't turn around. The stranger stays. His name is Wacholder. A reliable name, a man you can count on. He stays and stays. Talks and talks. With her. Talks nonsense and not to me. And he too goes. Now they're both gone. I'm sorry for my mother. First she was jealous, now she has lost two men and I'm sorry for her. Soon after, my mother went away too. Died. I'm alive, living with the same Wacholder, I despise him, I wish he were dead and I owe him everything. My false father, who always acted as if and even now he acts as if. With his crazy dreams and his miraculous cock and his foolery and his *idée fixe* about a woman he killed. Hadn't he just come out of her room, in his suspenders, with his shoes on? Did he lie on her like that, fully dressed? The way you lie on a whore? Then he went to wash, shave, freshen up and wash off the blood. Did he kill her? I'll never know. She died much later. And my childhood stopped. Doesn't interest me. Why write about it? I'm crying. Gorki cried too because his people were trampled, because they slept under straw roofs in the rain, because they lived in run-down shacks like me, because they lived like animals under the open sky with crazy people like me. Gorki cried and comforted them, so I'm entitled to cry too. For the same people. Alone in the cities and poor. We lived in the house he assigned to us in a tenement behind the Nevski Prospect. On the fifth floor. With a view on a backyard where drunks sleep, where murderers hide, waiting for the police or a miracle. Old people came into the yard to eat out of garbage pails, here children were born, the sick died, little children were raped by five little thugs. Instead of Gorki, Wacholder remained. He has a thing or two on his conscience. I am his pen.

Cautiously, so as not to damage his pages, he put them into the envelope and locked them up in the drawer. He turned the key twice. Wacholder rummaged all over. One of these days he might come across the five pages of *The Better World*. Aslan could only proceed on that assumption. To protect his own book, his private secret, he had been copying out the books of dead authors for several years. Wacholder suspected nothing.

Aslan: Do you know *Faust*, Father?

Which Faust? Mine is called Franz.

Mine is by Goethe. My pseudonym.

Wacholder: Can I take your word for that?

Aslan: Ask Leo.

Wacholder: Leo, is Aslan Goethe? I've known him a long time, and this is the first I've heard of it.

Leo: You didn't know? I'm amazed. Aslan has lots of pseudonyms. More than you'll ever meet.

Wacholder: What are pseudonyms?

Leo: Well, Goethe, Schiller, Kleist, Heine and Edgar Wallace, for instance, are pseudonyms for Aslan. You see, he wrote them all.

Wacholder: All those famous men are my Aslan? Is that true, Aslan?

Yes, Father, I'm very famous. That's why I don't go to town very often. People recognize me first thing. Hi, Johann Wolfgang, or Good morning, Friedrich. I don't care for familiarity. Those people who greet me because I've written a few classics aren't real friends. They wouldn't even say hello to me.

When did you write those things? You never tell me anything.

When? Year in, year out. This year, for instance, I wrote Hegel. That wasn't easy.

What did you write him?

I am Hegel.

And you wrote yourself that you're Hegel? Don't you talk to yourself like me, like all normal people? Do you have to write to yourself?

Writing to myself is nothing. The crux is what I write. The book. I'm famous, but at heart I'm a Rumpelstiltskin.

Did you write that too, Aslan? It doesn't matter, the main thing is getting rid of the paper.

It's safe with me. Thomas Mann's *Goose of Lübeck* is mine too. Posthumous.

What else?

The Paradox by Chamonis. A writer little known here, born in Peru in 1859, spent his life in Paris. A friend of Zola and Apollinaire and Proust and Gide.

And you're he?

The opening sentence of *The Paradox* is marvelous. Listen. There is no such thing as a paradox, because everything is paradoxical. Isn't that good? It's better than Leo.

Couldn't you be the Frenchman from Peru without writing *The Paradox*? Or write *The Paradox* under your own name? Do you ever write under the name of Aslan? Leo writes as Leo.

Nothing that anybody ever heard of or bought. But people are willing to pay for my handwritten Goethe. It's very rare.

And what will you do when you're done with Hegel?

I'll write all the C's. Cafka, Cleist, Cervantes, Çola, Céline.

Don't bother us with your Çola. Are you Cervantes or not?

Yes, Father, I'm he. You guessed it. Pure luck.

Good. The main thing is to get rid of the paper.

After one of these conversations Wacholder flew into a rage. That's all stupid, he screamed. I shit on your stupidity, what good is it to me, I'm stupid enough without your nonsense. Everybody can hoodwink me because I'm a simple man, that's the whole trouble. Just leave me in peace. Write what you like, but not a word about me. I don't let anybody write about me. Because I know myself best. What you and Leo dream up is nonsense. I'm not going to let anybody ruin my health. Certainly not you two. I am I. There's nothing else like me. When I compare my I and other people's I, I've got to laugh. You won't find an I like mine anywhere. Other people think they've got an I, but look at them.

That's no I, it's not even a We. It's nothing. Nothing may be an exaggeration. Everybody has a tiny I, even the most primitive man has a little drop of We. If he didn't he'd get lost, because he wouldn't belong to anybody. He'd turn to some kind of street mongrel with a We-vitamin shortage. Take a look at the world. Is that a world? You could almost say it's a waste of time looking at the world, because it isn't one. So between you and me, don't look at the world, it's indescribable anyway. There's no point in describing this world, but do as you please. The main thing is to get rid of the paper.

Thirty tons of confiscated white paper lay between spiral staircase and kitchen. A long journey over lakes and mountains, ending in the garbage can. Paper. Paper.

Wherever you looked, paper. Neither Aslan nor Leo could use it all up with their writing. Wacholder, for his part, did his best. He slept in the paper (Leo: He's eating his way through it), chewed on it, sold it to junk dealers, tore whole reams of it when he was in a bad humor, folded it into kites and boats and gave them to children, supplied the chestnut vendors with bags, sopped up puddles with paper, gave it to the kitchen gardeners free of charge for their seeds and bulbs, and exchanged it at the grocer's for plums and grapes. And couldn't get rid of it. The white mountain was a blind eye that wouldn't let anyone close it. The paper had been there from all eternity, it would cease only with the end of the world, and sometimes it seemed to him that he had been born here of a paper father and a paper mother, and he himself made of paper.

Ah yes, ah yes
I'm really glad, ah yes,
to see you here so beautiful,
ah yes, ah yes, my precious hair,
today you're really beautiful.

Next door in Room 5 Rita was combing the horsehair of the mattresses, as she did every third Tuesday; lovingly she removed the curly hair from the mattress, tenderly she stretched it out under leather straps in a table built for that purpose. Today she is singing a song. Only a little ditty, sung in an untrained voice, but it sounds familiar like a nursery rhyme. They had made up this song together. Each had contributed a word, a syllable, a snatch of melody. They had no son, but they had this "Ah Yes." Rita had two sons by her first marriage, her marriage with Ossias had produced nothing of the kind. The "Ah Yes" was resignation and reproach, but sometimes it also sounded heroic.

Würz, on his bed, listened to the familiar ditty with closed eyes, and he felt sorry for Rita. Something new would have to happen, some joyful surprise. I must do something new (he hardly dared to think it)—begin a new life, for instance. Yes, a new life, that's the least I can do for her. Laugh. That's it. I must learn to laugh, to laugh, to be gay. That would be nice, it would be funny too. To laugh gaily, a boisterous ha-ha laugh. For fear of being overheard, Würz pulled the blanket over his head and tried to make his face laugh. At first it cost him a violent effort, but little by little it came more naturally. Easy does it. He raised his upper lip, spread his lips till his cheeks hurt, half closed his eyes and began to cough. It was only a beginning, but the face was right, that's the way people laugh, exactly. Then with the second hand of his pocket watch he tried to time an average and above-average laugh. To simplify matters, he divided the operation into phases. Phase 1 took ten seconds, Phase 2 thirty seconds, and Phase 3 sixty seconds. When he succeeded for the fourth time in attaining Phase 3, he was pretty well satisfied with the result. Actually, three times was enough, but as usual in important undertakings, he wanted to build up a reserve. The only trouble was that he couldn't decide when and where he would apply this new exercise of the facial muscles, as he called it. He certainly had nothing to laugh about. He thought of the celebration, of Rita's sons, who grew more sullen every day, and over and over again of Antidust, the magnetic dust remover he had fallen for, and reproached himself.

How can I, how could I? I'm fifty-five years old and still lightheaded. I'm a victim of credulity. I'm a lamb. All salesmen are scoundrels. They're all sly and cynical, and I'm only a plain simple man. They're highway robbers, pirates, hardened criminals, hyenas, I'm only a dwarf pinscher, and that's what comes of it. To Würz, Antidust, the magnetic dust remover—the foreign name alone was a sure sign—was a plot designed to rob him, him personally, of his hard-earned money and to make him a laughingstock to boot. For it was perfectly clear that dust which does not settle remains suspended in midair. Dust that isn't localized and visible hovers invisibly everywhere. A mysterious cloud of invisible infinitesimal particles, pure poison to the lungs.

In his own home he had been battling the invisible evil of this world for seventeen years. Was that a laughing matter? It had taken him three weeks to get to the bottom of it, three weeks that seemed like three hundred years. Long ago the machine had been stored away in Room 2, but the damage was more than financial, it was spiritual and im-

measurable. How long would it be before the last grain of
dust stirred up by that diabolical contraption would dis-
close itself to the eye? The manufacturers couldn't say.
They had broken off the correspondence, leaving Würz
and his dust to their fate, and in this fate Würz tossed
restlessly this way and that. Yesterday's blood and stool
samples had revealed a sorry picture. The decisión to in-
stall special electric stoves had been adopted unanimously
at Sunday's family conference. On Monday, Arnulf had
raised doubts. On Sunday they had decided on drastic and
immediate measures against the dust still suspended in the
air. Destroy it, he had proclaimed, burn it without delay.
And on Monday, Arnulf comes up with his objection, driving Würz back to his very last trench.

What about the smoke, Father, not the smoke from
our chimneys that blows over to the neighbors, no need to
worry about that; I mean the smoke that escapes from the
open door of the stove. What about that, Father?

Würz had no answer. I don't know, Arnulf, he said
finally. We need an electric stove.

But can we rely on electricity, Father?

Of course the lout is right. The smoke from the stove
door, the smoke from the stove door. After he had repeated these words twenty times, until the whole family
was shouting Smoke from the stove door in chorus, he
came out with his last argument, and he wasn't at all
happy about it. Providence, he cried, some things must be
left to providence. We do our best. After every incinera-
tion we take a hot bath. Plenty of soapsuds. plenty of
water, what more can we do, nothing more is possible.

Providence, God, my loved ones. The power of God, he shouted still louder. In the hand of God, he roared, and didn't believe a word of it. The business with the special stoves was definitely a defeat, that had become clear. But dirt is our misfortune, the misfortune of us all, don't you see that?

The city is damp, no doubt about it. The river, the plain, the awful climate. Bronchitis and asthma, the constant drizzle. Everywhere mold and decay. Another man would have made his peace with the facts. But Würz was made of different stuff. Rain is rain, he said. There may be some truth in that. But it's not just the climate. The people around here like to harp on the weather. Everything that's no good in our city is called weather. What about man? To keep pretexting the weather is a pretext. People lie, even to themselves. When will they recognize the truth? Yes, yes, nature is nature, and climate is climate. But man is neither one nor the other. Man is ruler over nature, its tamer. Man is everything, nature is only his garden. A garden that has to be spaded and weeded constantly. Nature means work, everyone must do his share. Let each man do his best. Even if it takes a whole lifetime to civilize a corner of this jungle—a two-story house in a secluded street, for instance—my work will not have been wasted. With the humblest labor, if you go about it intelligently, you will have done something for the salvation of this world.

That was the philosophy of Ossias Würz. It was neat

and clean, the heritage of many generations of Protestant pastors and artisans, it was bright and purified like every fiber of his curtains, which were protected by specially designed plastic curtain-protector curtains.

Würz didn't laugh, because when you come right down to it, he had nothing to laugh about, not even on a morning when a laugh would have meant a good deal to him.

I don't laugh because I mustn't and shouldn't laugh, though I ought to.

With an effort, he stood up from his bed and stepped in front of the large mirror on his clothes cupboard. Self-purification by confrontation—that was the purpose of his striptease before the mirror. If you wish to see the truth, the Gypsy woman had advised him for five schillings, undress in front of the mirror, take off everything, even your watch, and see the truth as you should see it. Look at yourself like that for fifteen minutes, concentrate on yourself, the mirror never lies. What stands before you is you. You'll see.

This private and intimate exhibition took the place of confession and psychiatry. Here I stand, Ossias Würz, aged fifty-five, a man in his middle years, no beauty-prize winner. I have one, two, three, four, five, six, seven, eight, nine, ten toes, I have one, two, three, four, five, six, seven, eight, nine, ten fingers. I have two arms, two legs and a trunk. I have a male sex organ of average size, and testicles corresponding. I have two protuberant eyes, they explore space; nothing can escape them. I have a nose (he grasped his nose), large, broad and round. Yes, my stomach is there. Navel there. Yes. He turned his back to the mirror and looked over his shoulder: back, behind, heels, all complete. My carrot-colored hair is hideous (he tugged at his hair). But it's there, and that's the main thing. Everything's there, therefore I'm here. Existence established.

Having laid the groundwork for profounder reflections by establishing his existence, he continued his self-examination. Pulled his lower eyelids down, stuck out his tongue, tugged at his ear lobes to have a closer look, breathed three times quickly through his nose and said, Good, breathing all right; stuck his forefinger in his navel, weighed his testicles in one hand, slapped his right knee with the flat of his hand and spread out his toes.

The spiritual inventory could now begin. He repeated the words: Here am I, Ossias Würz, aged fifty-five, a man in his middle years, no beauty-prize winner. Then suddenly he remembered the rectal test. Quickly he stuck his right forefinger up his anus, smelled it, and satisfied with the smell, he could now go on. I am the son of my father, the son of my mother, the grandson of my grandparents. My wife's husband, my sons' stepfather, without profession, residing at Melchiorstrasse No. 9.

That's that. How am I, Ossias Würz? Happy? At first he hesitated, then he said aloud: No, not happy. Very well then, come to the point: what's wrong with me?

Restless?

Am I confused?

Yes, I am confused.

Did Wacholder's letter upset me again?

It always does, it hurts me.

But didn't I tell him off?

No, I'm not satisfied with that answer.

Did I neglect to say something I should have said?

Should or could, what do I mean?

Both.

Well, what is it?

No, I won't say.

Then I will.

No, I won't.

For the last time I must tell myself the truth. I can trust myself. I won't betray myself. I'll keep my secret. I ought to tell myself what I ought to tell myself. If I promise myself on my word of honor never to give myself away, never to tell anyone, not a soul, not even in my sleep, then it's all right for me to tell myself. Well?

A dog.

What? A dog?

Yes. A dog.

Me a dog?

Yes, I'm a dog.

Not a tree-stump goblin, not a banana peel, but a dog?

Yes, that's what I am. Between you and me. A dog. Can't prove it, but I know it.

Do I know what I'm saying?

Not always, but this time definitely. Don't I remember what he called me once?

What did he call me?

Dog!

And I believe that? Do I believe that he really doesn't

like me? Do I believe that his inviting me to Greenland is only a pretext to lure me out of my house and catch me and sell me to an asylum? That pig.

Yes, unfortunately, I believe it.

So I believe that he's not really my friend. Unbelievable, but now it's clear.

Does he hate me then?

Yes, he hates me and wants to destroy me.

Am I not imagining that?

No. No. He wants to lure me to Greenland, and there, where no one can see it, or ever hear about it, he wants to kill me or to tie me to his sled.

Harness me to his sled? Is that possible?

Why not? And drag me around the landscape with bells around my neck?

Bells on my neck? What a crazy idea.

That's how it is. I'll have to sound his bells. As if I were his church. But I'm not his church. Nor his chapel. I'm not a dog, and certainly not a sled dog.

But what about Greenland? Don't I want to go there, where everything is peaceful and clean?

Yes, I suppose I do.

Well then, do I want what I really want, or don't I want what I really want? Do I love the pure snow, cleanliness, or don't I? It's high time I told myself.

I never love what I love.

Then do I hate what I love?

No. I don't even hate what I love.

Do I at least hate what I hate?

I never hate what I hate. I neither hate what I love nor

love what I hate. On the other hand, I don't hate what I hate either, and I'm not capable of loving what I love. But I've said that already.

So what am I doing. Who am I? Do I know who I am? Do I understand myself?

Do I understand myself?

But if I don't know where I'm at, who does? Who am I then?

He stood bolt upright, pressing the palms of his hands against his thighs, and said: I am Ossias Würz, fifty-five, a man in his middle years, but I know that already, and I hate Wacholder. That's definite. But since I neither hate nor love what I hate or love, because that kind of thing is simply beyond me, everything is all the same to me, not only for that reason but in general.

Do I mean, Würz asked himself hesitantly, screwing up his eyes, that same things are the same to me? He had to repeat the question.

Of course same things are the same to me, he said, breathing a sigh of relief, just as different things are also the same and different things are not the same, but I've already said that.

Is that all? I must tell myself everything. Conceal nothing.

But I am telling everything. I tell myself everything I tell myself, the rest is hidden.

I have no right to do that to me. Hiding something I know from myself, won't do. If I still have any secrets from myself, I'm going to tell them now.

The dog.

Which dog this time?

The same. The sled dog.

The one I don't want to be?

No, the one I want to be.

Do I really want to be Wacholder's sled dog. I'm not ashamed of myself?

No, I'm not ashamed. I want to be not only Wacholder's but everybody's sled dog, and take every burden on myself, because that's the way I am. I want to drag everything across snow, ice, mountains and crags; jump from floe to floe, I'd like that.

I would?

Yes, I really would.

And what do I expect to gain by it?

Gain? Nothing. I want to suffer.

To suffer like a saint?

To suffer like Jesus Christ?

Am I Jesus? Do I want to be Christ?

Yes, I want to be He, and I am. And not only He. Not only the worshiped. I want to worship too. I want to be He and we and those who don't pray.

He, we, they and I?

And you, of course.

Why you?

Because you are different.

Then if I were everyone in the singular and in the plural, then would I be happy?

Yes and no. Because, to tell the truth, I want to be everyone in the past and future as well.

Is that all?

No. Not quite. Male and female.

But why?

To be complete. Because I think there'd be something missing if I were only a third person singular masculine, for instance.

What is missing?

She, of course.

Who?

Me, of course. In the first person singular it's not so important, it only gets embarrassing in the third. I insist on being both third persons in the singular and plural, past and future. I know I don't make things easy for myself, I'm not an easygoing man. Or a heavygoing one either (Würz twinkled an eye at himself). Between you and me, I'm not a man at all, I'm Wacholder's sled dog.

But am I not Wacholder too?

Sometimes, to tell the truth, yes.

And He? The Saviour.

Yes, I've already said yes to that. As Christ, I wish to cover myself with church bells and tie myself to my Wacholder's sled and run across the ice with myself, exploring Greenland.

But where am I going?

Wherever I take myself. I'll go here and there. I'll go everywhere. To someplace where the world ends, where it simply can't go on. I have to stop somewhere.

Why not here and now?

Not here.

But in Greenland, right?

Greenland, yes, it's easier there because I . . . because I myself am Greenland.

I thought I was the dog with the church bells, dragging himself as Christ across the ice.

Myself or himself?

Myself, myself.

No, of course I'm Greenland too, because otherwise, as Wacholder with Christdog, I couldn't hope to find true solitude. Of course I am Greeland, the ice, the snow, the mountains and the crags, the crevices, the floes and the sea.

I never told myself that before.

But now I know. I am the bell-ringing ice landscape which drives Christ over Wacholder, who as a dog is trotting ahead of my sled as all persons, male and female, in the present, now in the past then, and also in the future forever, and, who knows, perhaps even in the past indefinite.

Exhausted by so much curiosity, Würz went over to the bed. He wanted to lie down, but he had overlooked something in the dialectic of his own existence. Body motion. His own stiffness frightened him. He had to bend, bend forward and backward, double up and stretch, spin his trunk, rotate his head and fling his legs back, faster, faster, as though running, but without stirring from the spot, body bent far forward, swing elbows faster, breathe correctly. That does it.

He lay on the bed, staring at the ceiling, contented, as

though he had just swallowed himself and could feel himself in his own stomach. Rita came in with rags, ladder and gasoline.

5 The naked man on the bed (who looked very much like her Ossias, maybe he actually is Ossias, with him you never know) pointed his little friend at her instead of his digit, directed her up the ladder with the pink plump finger. He's funny again today. Rita wanted to laugh aloud but restrained herself. He didn't care for her "vulgar giggling." Würz was still lying open-mouthed, drowned. He stared upward to where white and black formed a triangle, and most of all (so it seemed to her) he'd have liked to look into her belly. She looked down at him, she wanted to turn that gaze of his aside. Now Würz was looking at her white plastic gloves. Above the third knuckle of her right hand. Wasn't there a spot? She saw no spot. Würz's eyes crept over her bosom, grazed her left cheek, paused a quarter of a second at the left nostril, found nothing of interest, and stopped at the brim of the broad Panama that she usually wore when the ceiling was to be cleaned. Again the brim wasn't turned down enough to suit him. Watch out for the lime. Protect your hair. Slips down the back of your neck into your dress. Careful.

With the help of long rulers, the ceiling had been divided into ten-centimeter squares, each of which was numbered. That, according to Würz, was the only way of doing the work systematically and thoroughly. Holding a piece of cotton in her strong stubby fingers, Rita soaked it in gasoline and started on the first square. Her white fingers moved regularly back and forth, a strange, long-legged insect whose head had been struck off. She found it hard to concentrate. Ossias dazzled her. That whiteness with the red head and pubic hair gave her the creeps, but disconcerted her less than his open-mouthed silence. A fish holding his head out of the water, while she herself flew about the room, a bird not interested in this kind of food.

Avoiding his eyes, she thought of the seventeenth-anniversary celebration that the silly fool insisted on. And what happens at these parties?

The four of us sit around the living-room table. Ossias makes a long, unintelligible speech, you raise your glasses and drink just a little. You cut into a cake. You nibble a bit of it. You look at each other and say nothing, ten minutes, half an hour. You mustn't break the silence, this is a solemn celebration. A serious affair. The boys will yawn and stretch out their feet under the table, that means trouble.

She will have to admonish them with a stern glance. In the end Father will stand up, shake hands with each of them, and wishing them three loud good nights, disappear with a solemn step into his room. Last year, just to put a little life into the party, she had told the story about the prunes. And what happened? Naturally he had interrupted her with a sharp: Nonsense, Rita. Then he had claimed the story was entirely different. Thinks he knows it all. How can he know? The story comes from the Hauches, not from the Würzes. Würz? What kind of a name is that? Würz, why not Wart? Würz-Wart. Luckily his name isn't Wart, but it must have been before, he must have had it changed. Würz suits him, he made a good choice. But Ossias is bad. Who calls himself Ossias? Oswald, all right. Oskar in a pinch, but Ossias? Maybe that was a fake name too, maybe it used to be Ottokar, that's what he looks like, or even Ottoman, it would be just like him.

I'm a Hauch, a real Hauch, the Hauches are a family with character, they put up with a lot, but they forget nothing. For a while they say Yes, very well. But one fine day they are perfectly capable of saying No, nothing doing. I am a Hauch, with my own family tree and roots. He'd better not rile me.

Würz had other things to think about than riling Rita, black-and-white Rita, who was scraping the ceiling and hanging from it by her fingers. Wacholder's letter, the cat, the summer morning, and the nausea that regularly set in after his inventory at the mirror. When I can't stand it any more, I'll scream. Like that other time. On March 12, when they pulled me out of my mother and beat me. All on account of that hand. Just wanted to feel for half a second what it was like outside, but I wasn't born yet. My mother screamed, her relatives called the doctor. A hemorrhage in the ice. The colors of the flag in the room. New life is a winter. I'd have waited another nine months. But they caught me. There was no going back. There was a stink, and then they hauled off at me. The big hit the little, and the defenseless are at the mercy of cold and hunger. Whichever way you looked, there were things to eat. Pink meat, hairy meat, raw meat, roasted meat. On all sides, cheeks, noses, lips and necks, breasts, thighs, arms and cocks. A big family. And what do they give me? Rancid milk, crushed vegetables, and they laugh, they laugh at me. The little fellow's a big eater, ha ha, lives on vegetable leavings and spoiled milk, ha ha. A clout on the back that drives the wind out of all your openings. You take a little bite out of the Celluloid duck, right away they turn your stomach inside out, you swallow some glass beads, they do it again. Greedy fingers snatch the coins and buttons out of your diapers. But never mind the carrots, you can keep them.

The carrots colored his hair, they didn't mind. A red-head from birth. There goes Redhead . . . Look, Redhead's coming . . . Everything about me is red. My fingers, my nails, I have red eyes and red teeth. A bright red electric sign. I am red Ossias Würz. Over there Wacholder is sleeping in his wastepaper basket, while I sleep in my castle. And both of us are lost. I don't go out and I won't let him in. Rita hangs from the ceiling, and our sons are prowling in the thicket outside. Rita, drop everything and jump! Rita hesitated. She wasn't sure. I have my character. I mustn't give in.

Jump, Rita!

I am I, Rita said to herself, and repeated the sentence to herself on every rung. I am I, Ossias, she said aloud when she stood by the bed beside him. What can I do for you?

It!

The Würzian acts took roughly half an hour. Afterwards they hid them in underwear, shirts and dresses, and put them aside until further notice. Good, excellent. Fine and dandy. And now?

Postpone the celebration, Ossias, till another time.

But this time I have a surprise, Rita, I can't tell you about it yet.

Rita laced the ladder's little woolen slippers and climbed up again. In that case, I have a surprise too, Ossias. His jaws went stiff, the palms of his hands were damp. Don't do anything foolish, Rita, he called up to her. The city is a labyrinth. Everybody goes round and round and thanks God if some Wacholder takes him into his rat cage. Here we already know where we are. We have two rooms in the basement, two on the ground floor and four on the second floor. On the third floor we have another four bedrooms. We have a house. The rooms are numbered, we have order. In every room an inventory is posted, like in the train. What more do you want, Rita? We have a beautiful, orderly, clean home. What more do we need? Tell me, and I'll get it.

The boys, Ossias, the boys.

Oh yes, the boys. It's always the boys. They're eighteen and twenty, not children any more. They've got to work like everybody else. Like all of us.

He withdrew into his closet. A few minutes later he stepped out in white overalls, white shoes and white gloves, on his head a white crash helmet, on his face a white gas mask, and went to Workshop 2 in the cellar for paint and brushes. To paint the walls in Room 14 . . .

6 He dragged himself across the Reichs Bridge to his shed and knew: nothing will come of it. It was the seventy-fourth answer to his seventy-fourth letter. A waste of stamps. A waste of ink. A waste of everything. It was even too bad about the paper. Either you do something or you do nothing, but this writing back and forth has to stop. It has stopped. This was the last letter and this was the last answer, and now something's got to happen, because it's high time. The time comes when you have enough, when your own friendliness gets on your nerves, and even if you have the friendliest nature in the world—like me, for instance—you've got to draw the line somewhere. Too much is enough. It won't go on like this, because it can't go on like this. The passers-by on the bridge avoided him, described a circle around this man talking to himself. For a time Wacholder looked grave and sullen, then he looked happy and serene, and he didn't talk out loud to himself uninterruptedly. Some of the time he thought with pressed lips of Aslan and Leo and what they would say. You and your idealism, Leo will scoff. Yes, yes, Aslan will say, and after long urging another Yes, yes. Yes, yes is easily said. They don't realize how dangerous that Würz is, sitting over there in his house. They just don't understand. Maybe such things simply can't be understood. You have to know.

You mustard pickle, Leo would shout, you'll have to invent something entirely different for Würz, you'll have to invent something that doesn't exist. Letters won't do any good with him. Then Aslan butts in. That angleworm. I understand you, Father, I know what you mean. Out here with us, in normal life, everything is topsy-turvy, back and forth, up and down at once. That's what normal life is like. But Würz is living in the fourth dimension. He's drawn a circle around himself.

And he talks about values too, Wacholder interrupts. Values are words, you don't have to take him at his word. He's cowardly, fanatical and backward. A man like that can say anything he likes. He's a fool, a jackass.

Yes, Leo, you've caught on, Wacholder cried out (a passing woman turned around and laughed in his face). And because he's cowardly and fanatical and backward, he's also a public menace. Do you know what's he's cooking up over there? You don't and I don't. But I'll tell you one thing: that constant cleaning and painting leaves me no peace. Are you sure he's not dreaming up something over there that will do me in? And that doesn't concern only me, it concerns all of us!

Naturally Aslan tries to calm him down: Forget him, Father, he won't meddle in our business.

That shows what a blockhead Aslan is. We haven't got any business, you sap, that's why he won't meddle in it. Doesn't have to. His presence is meddling enough. He threatens me. One of these days he'll come along with a pickax and knock me . . .

That would suit you, wouldn't it? Leo laughs.

No, no, there's no talking with you people.

Wacholder preferred to stick to his companion, his twin brother (whom he always seemed to confuse with Würz), whose slightest move struck him as more intelligent than his two friends' most lucid disquisitions. He followed his companion's most trifling actions with mounting anxiety. What is he doing? What is he up to? What is my Siamese twin thinking? Is he tired now? Is he moody, disgruntled. Where is he going? My poor blind brother. I'll buy you a yellow arm band with three dots and tie you to a white cane. Would you like that? Yes, one of these days I'll have to make you learn something sensible. Should I buy you a dog? Don't keep shaking your head. You say no to everything I suggest. Stop shaking your head like that. You sanctimonious bastard, you're putting on, I know you, and you know my weaknesses, you want to use me, to ruin me, you scum. That prick is going to be the death of me.

He bent over the iron rail and stared down into the dark water, seeing nothing. His blind brother had let go his hand. Wacholder sank into foam and bubbles. Foam, soft water, soft foam. That foam seeps into your brain, it gets on your nerves. Take it away!

Nerve foam. Nerve foam.

Nerve foam.

That's what I'll do to Würz. I'll get him; I'll get him with air, with thousands of bubbles. With brain poison. Watch it, Würz. Here it comes. Through the water pipes, gushing from every faucet. Hot from the hot and cold from the cold. That'll show him how to clean house. First he'll be surprised, then he'll go mad. *Whish.* Wacholder smiled. *Whish swish. Whish* and *swish.* He shouted so loud that even motorists turned around. I've got it.

The nerve shower. That'll wash the snail out of the house and wash the dirt in. A lovely white tickly nerve shower, won't that be nice? Or should I have it colored? I can make it colored too. He bored his index finger into the heart of the next passer-by, a young man with a slanting head and a briefcase. What do you think? Red? Purple? Pink? Or blue-green?

The young man gave him a frightened look and hastily retreated a few steps. Wacholder went on unhindered. He was very happy now. The brain tincture was a splendid idea, he decided. At first I'll keep it white, even that's quite an accomplishment. His happiness lasted three minutes, then the world went dark before his eyes. Worries. Practical considerations. How will I get a water pipe? I can't send him the juice in a truck. It'll all escape before it gets there. No, it's got to go through the water system, it's got to rise up unexpectedly from deep down, that's right, it's got to come from way down deep.

Wacholder saw Würz running out of his house, crying Help! Help! He saw the juice gushing under high pressure from every faucet in the house. He saw the fire department at work with long hoses. I'll put one over on you, he shouted with enthusiasm. Just wait. I'll get you yet. You'll come out of there. You'll come out all right.

Now Wacholder was raving. He walked faster and faster, in the end he was running, shouting uninterruptedly: You with your peaceful labor, you progress bug, you builder of the future. A goldbrick, that's what you are. I've come to set you free. People ran after him on the bridge. They thought he was a political agitator, maybe he wanted to free Hungary from the Communists. Anyway something to look at. I'm not going to beg and plead forever, not I! I'm going to act. Action delivered to your home by the municipal water department. You asked for it. You'll sit up and take notice, whether you want to or not. Wacholder's step slackened, he began to mutter: How am I going to scare up a water-department man in a hurry? I can't dig up a pipe without permission. There'd be hell to pay. You've got to do these things officially, by bribery or glib talk. By now his whisper was scarcely audible: But whom can you talk into a thing like that nowadays? And with prices what they are, whom can you bribe for a hundred schillings?

What's a hundred schillings anyway? Wacholder whimpered. Two tickets to the movies or three packs of cigarettes. One or the other. No, it can't be done for money. That leaves only the power of persuasion. (Wacholder put on a domineering look, but changed it at once to friendly.) Be nice. That's it, I've got to be nice. Find somebody from the water department (a sly look) in a

restaurant, or maybe in a café, playing cards. Flatter him.
(He bent down, said Wheedle, wheedle, and grinned.)
Take an interest in him, or rather in his family. Get personal, so to speak. But only so to speak, where would we
be if we began doing that kind of thing in earnest? Today
everybody is lonely. We have a mass society, so the individual is lonely. The more people there are, the lonelier
people get. I'll have to make friends. Abase myself. (What
I won't do for that lousy Würz!) And then little by little,
it's all in the game, first take the children for a walk, treat
them to chocolate, give them piggyback rides, and after
three four visits, when I'm practically a member of the
family and we're calling each other by our first names, I'll
say: Come to think of it, Franz, could you do me a little
favor? In passing, while watching television. When you
get a chance, of course, there's no hurry. You see, I have
this friend, name of Würz, on Melchiorstrasse, I'd like to
give him a little surprise, he's a joker, see, he likes a little
joke, just for fun, see, I'd like to blow some kind of nerve
medicine through his water pipes. See? He'd get a kick out
of it. You open up the pipe someplace, you'd know the
best place, and I pour in two three bottles of my medicine,
and when this joker opens the faucet, he gets it *whish
swish* in the face. He'd die laughing. Wouldn't that be a
lark?

What kind of nerve medicine? Franz asks.

How serious people are nowadays, like German writers.
What kind of nerve medicine? What a question. How
should I know so early in the game? That's not so easy to
explain. Why do you have to get so serious right away?

People take everything so seriously nowadays. No, it was different in the old days. Things have changed. That comes from the years of misunderstanding, that comes from Hitler.

Wacholder walked more and more slowly, sauntered down Schüttenstrasse deep in thought, and suddenly, quite unexpectedly, found himself face to face with One-Ear Wondra in the Other World.

At that time of year Wondra stood outside St. Joseph's, where the No. 24 streetcar describes a loop, across from the Central School for Boys and only ten doors away from the Habsburg Steam Laundry. In the winter he sold chestnuts, in the summer newspapers. The clouds of smoke from the laundry chimneys and the river mist that hung in the air at all times of year gave the neighborhood its name: the Other World. Where other people have their right ear, Wondra had a finger, actually it was only a child's fingertip. Nailless and pink. A sausage end, a blister, a next-to-nothing. Hence, One-Ear Wondra. A good fellow, the kind you could talk to, because he liked best to do the talking himself. A human chestnut and newspaper vendor, well liked throughout the neighborhood. Like the one-fingered, the short-armed, the legless, the harelipped and the deaf-blind, Wondra of the one ear was highly esteemed. Most people had only good to say of him, and often praised him for no reason. They said: Wondra will help you. They said: Have a cry on Wondra's shoulder. Because his infirmity was so evident, people felt that he had met his debt to original sin at birth. His friendliness seemed abnormal. Only the malicious said bad things about him, some claimed he had cut off his ear when the war broke out. Since he was usually in a good humor, they doubted his sincerity. One often heard statements such as: He knows what he's doing. Or: Whichever way Wondra spins, he always comes down on his ear. Which was really malicious, because naturally the left side of Wondra's face was heavier.

To Wacholder this Wondra was "a man you could talk to." Not a friend, but at least a human being. What kind of sauce should I make him? Colored or white? What do you think? Wondra stretched, spread his fingers, balled them into fists and pounded the newspapers, as though you could change history by pummeling the headlines. Here was someone wanting to strike up a conversation, what mattered was not who he was, but the fact that someone had come to talk.

Hello, Wacholder, d'you hear what happened to me yesterday? No? The business with Bunzig. You haven't heard—

What color, Wondra? White or colored?

Anyway, this Bunzig, this run-down count, this degenerate with the ingrown monocle, has been at it again. Making a stink. Right here in front of all the people. Comes around complaining that his ad for a housekeeper isn't in the paper.

This water, Wondra, I've been thinking about it a long time, say, I've been thinking, that *is* a good idea. Well, so long.

So long, Wacholder, you going so soon? Wait till I've finished my story. I say to this pimp— My dear count, I

47

say, what do I care about your ad? Call up the newspaper if you want to make a complaint.

No, he yells, so loud that the people all come running, no, Wondra, it's your fault. You're on the paper too. All the people on the paper are responsible.

I'm in chestnuts, I say, which isn't entirely a lie.

And what are these, my friend? he yells into my ear. Are these chestnuts?

First of all, I say, I'm not your friend. My friends are respectable people, not any bobtailed counts, and in the second place I'm in distribution. Advertising is in the city.

It's all one to me, he yells. Distribution, advertising. Anybody can say that. As far as I'm concerned, you're with the newspaper, and that's that.

What do you think of that? What an angry bastard. People around here get angry right away. The bourgeoisie are as bad as the nobles. It's supposed to be a sign of distinction. But I'm different. That kind of stuff won't go down with me. Beat it, I say. Blow, make tracks. Go back where you came from. You enemy of the workers, you exploiter, you and your floozy. It's no wonder we didn't print it, we don't accept pornographic ads.

I'm looking for a housekeeper, you earwig, he yells.

You know me, I'm good-natured, but I don't let anybody step on my sore point. I gave it to him good: Your housekeeper's a whore, an ugly run-down whore, you can lick my ass and so can she. I said it right to his face.

Okay, said Wacholder, the subject was getting too touchy for him. Get a load of this. Würz opens the faucet. He doesn't suspect a thing. And right away he gets it *whish swish* in the eyes. Will he sit up and take notice! He'll take notice all right, if he can see anything by that time.

Hello, Wacholder, you still here? Well, as long as you're here, stick around. As you see, I didn't beat about the bush, I gave him the truth, straight between the eyes. I don't believe in beating about the bush. Do you believe in beating about the bush?

Exactly, Wacholder cried out. The truth straight between the eyes. Ouch, he yells like a stuck pig. Ouch! What's this, who's done this to me? That's the purest truth. This brain soup in my clean home. Phooey!

Pipe down, Wacholder. The main thing is, you don't believe in beating about the bush either. Anyway, as far as I was concerned, the matter was settled. I turn around, there was a customer wanting to buy a paper, nobody buys papers any more these days, and no wonder, too much cheap sensationalism, so I turn my back on Bunzig, and a second later it's like I'm being strangled from behind. What do you think he'd done? I swear by all that's holy, he'd jumped up on my back. Let go, I yell, as well as you can yell when you're being choked, let go, I gasp, you damn fool, let go, who the devil do you think you are?

The Devil? he sings out. Karl-Maria Eduard Heinz Bunzig is sitting on your neck.

Let go, I bellow. The people take a few steps backward, but do you think anybody'd help me? You don't know our people. They stood there like cattle. Grinning. They thought it was some kind of show, and meanwhile he damn near killed me. He hugged me with all his might with both arms and locked his legs in front of my stomach.

Has that ever happened to you? Somebody locking his legs in front of your stomach? A perfect stranger—

Legs? Wacholder interrupted. The nerve tincture comes out of faucets, not legs.

I fight and struggle, but the bastard won't let go. I almost felt like Luther. Didn't he have a devil on his neck too? Anyway, he didn't let go.

Of course not. He was right, Wacholder cried out, I wouldn't let him go either. That wouldn't be a bad idea, I jump on his neck and hold him in a full nelson until he eats humble pie. Until he comes out with his secret. I'm telling you, Würz is plotting something against me. No, if I had him by the throat, I'd never let go.

The same with this nut, Wacholder. Either you see to it that my ad appears in the paper tomorrow morning, he croaks, or you'll carry me to the office. This minute. I'm not letting you go.

Wacholder shook his head. Naturally he didn't let go, would you have let go in his place? When you've got your enemy, you've got him. Well, I wouldn't have sat down on his back, I'd have pulled him out. Into the fresh air. Then I'd have put him down on his head, taken him by the feet and shaken him. Until his secret plan fell out on the pavement. Würz is dangerous, I tell you.

Listen here, Wacholder. Wondra grew suddenly grave and looked him in the eye. I'm telling you a story about something that happened to me last night, and you keep interrupting me. I'm talking now, understand, when I'm through, you can talk.

Impressed by these words, Wacholder didn't bat an

eyelash. Wondra frightened him with his next question. I ask you, what would you have done if a total stranger jumped on your back out of a clear sky?

I would have—

I'm not interested in what you would have. Don't tell me you'd have been able to shake him off, because that Bunzig is a leech. Bunzig is thin and wiry, I tell you. He may be seventy, but he's hale and hearty. That's from playing tennis. No, you'd have been stuck with him too. I had to carry him all the way up Schüttenstrasse, then I threw him off outside his door. He was satisfied. But get the picture. Everybody saw me. They laughed at me. And the whole time I pretend everything is all right—it's only a bet, I sing out—but in my heart I knew I'd never been so humiliated. We're a people of horsemen—yes, Wacholder, I saw it clearly as I was sweating my way up Schütten-strasse. In our country the thin sit on the fat. The light on the heavy. Because do you think I could have done the same? If I'd sat down on Bunzig, he'd have collapsed un-der my weight. That's the long and the short of it. There's a lesson in this for you. If we, the common people, don't watch our diet and don't play tennis and go on eating the first thing that comes along, we'll be horses and mules for the gentry. I'm an old Socialist, and I'll tell you this: the party leadership misled us. They got us the forty-hour week, they raised our living standards. Today food is not only cheap, it's within the reach of everybody. They were in cahoots with the capitalists. The people gained weight, and the individual got fat. We can't defend ourselves any more. We're too fat, see, too heavy. And the Sozis are actually proud of it.

Good Lord, it's just occurred to me. Würz has just written me—want to read the letter?—that he's been putting on weight. You say it makes you sluggish. Maybe you're right. Now I see why he can't go out. He eats too much, he's too well off. I'll tell you one thing, Wondra, if my wonder juice doesn't do the trick, never mind, I'll boycott him. I'll starve him out. I'll steal the vitamins out of his food, how I don't know yet, but there must be some way. For a while he won't notice anything, but in time he'll get thin as paper, so thin I'll be able to pull him out under the closed door. How, I don't know. I don't even know how to make cocoa. Aslan and Leo don't know either. To tell the truth, they don't know a damn thing. They're intellectuals, see what I mean.

I don't know either, Wacholder, but I know my back still aches. Take it from me, anything can happen to you around here. Did you want a newspaper?

No thanks, Wondra, I'll drop by another time. I'm in a hurry now.

Suddenly Wacholder was in a hurry. He turned into Floridsdorfer Landstrasse. Thinking was hard for him, but what the natives call meditating, a state between mulling and daydreaming, is inevitable in this town. The question of the water-department employee left Wacholder no peace. What would nerve foam be? Just words, in all probability. What else could a nerve foam be? A gush of words, gibberish, something outlandish and foreign, some kind of Hungarian. Something the speaker himself doesn't understand and the one he's talking to isn't suppose to understand either. But words, all the same. And he'd already sent him ten thousand of those. Just the same, it could only be words, but maybe a different kind. Harder words. More complicated sentences. Book words. The kind of words that poets and thinkers dream up. Not bad. Aslan's a poet, Leo's a thinker, we'll manufacture it together. Nerve shower? How did I think of that? You think up a word because the foam in the water gets on your nerves and a minute later you're seeing fire engines and waterworks. You look closer and it's Hungarian. Can I help it? It's not my fault. Somebody inside me made a slip of the tongue. A little mistake. I've got to do something to make him lose his mind. Manufacture words till he almost drowns in them. A flood of words, when he's up to his ears in it I'll send in a rescue party.

That's it, some kind of gushing water that affects the brain. That's what I had in mind. I knew it all along.

It was about six o'clock. A tired, tedious weekday, smelling of swamp and trees. The sky was skimmed milk. Briefcases and shopping bags passed at longer and longer intervals. Shop shutters made a loud *r*. Flies sitting on fruit. And everyone yawned. Everybody was tired and sad, with worry in his face. Worry as heavy and jagged as the gray cobblestones. Bumpy dark faces over which ran dogs and motorcars and children on bicycles, zigzagging through dry eyes. Drowned in his own confusion, Wacholder drifted down the avenue in the direction of his shed.

7 Aslan! Aslan! Where are you? Nothing stirred. Dead. A light upstairs. The bastard's asleep of course, and as usual with the light on. Leo. No sign of Leo either. Vanished into thin air. What will I do now?

A damp evening, the darkness fell quickly. It could have been autumn or winter. Drizzling and cold. He didn't like to be alone in this kind of darkness. It's full of ghosts and shadows and funny sounds, no, it's not for me. These winding staircases are funny too. It's as if you could see yourself going up. You don't get that with other staircases. This one winds so strangely. You've got to wind too, twist in all directions or you won't make it. He tried again: Leo! Leo! The *o* crept into the corrugated iron under the wood, ran into the nearest hole. And now Leo's gone too. That's what I get. The *o* was still sounding, a high-pitched buzz. Suddenly it turned to a long *n*, an insect, a gnat over water. With every step the *n* grew louder and fiercer. Who's calling *n*? *Nnn*. What does it mean? Who's making *n*'s in my house? The *n* in woman, the *n* in torn, the *n* in open. I tore her open all right, the whore. Taking money from a poor man. Cheating a poor devil like me out of his last cent. What a city! Houses wherever you look. Nothing

54

but houses, and in every one of them somebody living. And light burning. Only in my cave, that flea palace, there's never any light. There's no light because nobody's home. It's not my fault. I'm proud. So some whore comes over, whores always come over without being asked, and starts insulting me: Come on, sweetie darling, let's fuck. What you waiting for? You'll never get anybody else with that face. An ugly-looking tramp like you. Come on in. Forty cents. That's all I've got. Give it here. Right into her cunt, my last money. Vanished. Well, what are you standing around for? Think I'm a social worker? Open your fly, you lazy bastard. Expect me to wait on you for forty cents? Forty cents. I bet I'm the crummiest in town, can't you see I'm humpbacked and cross-eyed and worn down like a horeshoe and so dirty I stink? You don't even notice. I don't feel like washing. I won't wash again until my Jimmy comes back, he ran off with a fat mama with a big ass and left me flat. Hell, my hard-luck stories are none of your business. Right. They're none of my business. Let's have that cunt so I can dig out my investment. No. No? No. Are you crazy? Think I was born yesterday? You'll never get in with that tool. Not in mine. No thanks—say, get a look at that thing, it's not normal, that's not a prick, it's a chunk of meat, it's like an arm stump, I had a soldier like that one time, but his was where it belonged. He was wounded in the war. Were you? They ought to put you in the fun fair. No thank you, here's your dough and beat it. Beat it? You don't like it? I'm out of luck. Look how cute it is. Eighteen inches of Wacholder in your cunt, doesn't that appeal to you? All for forty cents. Go away. Leave me alone. Open up, I say, here I come. Open up, I say, to hell with the forty cents, they're gone anyway. They're inside. Running and jumping around the room, over the bed, into the closet. Come on out or you'll see action. Braces his foot against it, the door flies open. There was action, all right. Off with the dress, off with the garter belt. And now open up. Stinks like a shithouse. Good, now hold still. Where's my money? What's tinkling? Tinkling already? It slides fine. Nice and juicy. Another time? No. I say yes. No! No! Yes! Yes! It runs like the Danube Canal, so nice and warm, like a Turkish bath almost, phew, it stinks. Come, will you, now, no now . . . Go on, do it, will you, shoot, will you. Look how nice it is down there, look, Otto, you're in. Go on now, do it . . . No. What, you bitch, you won't? In? In! She's bleeding. Fine how-do-you-do. She's stopped breathing. Swat her one. Give her a clout. Come on now, don't be that way. What's the matter, you crazy? Get up. Get up. It can't be. It's not true, you're not dead. Get up, I tell you, get up. Christ, she's sagging. She's fainted. Water. Where do I find a glass around here? Water. Yes, water. Christ, is he red, you've been butchered, son. Blood. It won't run. A puddle. Water. The faucet won't open. Try the other. The other trickles. That'll never fill a glass. But she doesn't move, she lies there like a corpse. I throw the water in her face. Not so bad-looking with her mouth closed. Two sweet little blue eyes. And her hair isn't gray. Kind of crummy with her shriveled breasts and her bones sticking out, but there's no hump. Not so good, but not so bad either. That face! Like wax. Sheds water. Better wash sonny boy first. Where's the

towel? A little soap would help. Doesn't matter. Poor bastard. Another dry run. How can I stand it, how can I stand
it? Oh well, it's all one. Tonight before I go to sleep. In
the pillow. What do I need women for? Stick the money
up their cunt, and then they say good-bye and faint. She
hasn't fainted. She's gone. The way she lies there. Would
you believe it? She's dead. Stinking dead whore. Somebody's killed her. Why? Or why not? Who cares? An ugly
puss like that is meant to be bashed in. Why not? Look
how ugly she is. And money she wants too.

I haven't got a thing. Work is no good either. What
do you make? Those lousy shirts. The stink all day long.
The steam dries you out inside. Ten hours you stand at the
washboard, the little fellow rubs against the wood, you've
got time to think. Hands make shirts. The things I think
about, the people around here would be amazed if they
knew. The Sammies and Izzies with their black eyes.
Funny. And the funny smile they have. That smile. It's
too intelligent. But that's the way they are. They spit on a
man like me. Because I'm a bum and not one of them,
can I help it if I'm not one of them? I'd rather have been
a Jew in the first place. I respect them. Because they're
decent and self-respecting. Just take a look at a Jewish
home. Everything shipshape. Beautiful things, pictures all
over, and always neat and clean, that's for me. And my
place? Don't ask. A garbage dump. Three dollars a month.
Not fit for a dog. No bed. A mattress on the floor and a
couple of torn blankets, that's all. What do you expect for
three dollars? And our fine-feathered Jews? They have
homes. They get ahead in the world. Hats off to the Jews.

If they knew what's going on in my head: A typical goy, they'd say. Coarse and vulgar. With us Jews it's different, we don't think such things. We do it too, we're human too. Human? When I hear that word—human! Yes, but we have a civilization. We respect our sexual partners. Get a load of that. Respect their sexual partners. With me, in any case, your Jewish lordships, it's different. I'm only a goy, but at least they haven't cut anything off me. That's why I've got a big one. I don't let anybody cut marks in it, I don't need a mark. I won't run away, here I belong and here I am. A cock is to fuck, not to respect with, it's not a hat to wave good-bye with. It's a cannon, a battleship to attack the enemy with. Ram it in. Women are the enemy. Into the lousy women, the Jews, the whores, the cunts. Crank her up to two-fifty, boys.

Women are a rotten business. You want to, all right, but they won't let you. They take one look at you and say: No, not with me. Try somebody else. And I always thought, the bigger the better. Wrong. Nowadays they want a little runt that hops around a bit and rubs his match on the box, but not too hard, just a little, they let him shoot, but not too often. When she's through, she says: I've had enough, leave me alone. You can get down on your knees and beg. No soap. When a woman doesn't want to, she doesn't want to. There's no use trying. Better do it in the pillow. Well anyway, this one is dead. Dead and gone. She's ice-cold. Good-bye, lady. I'm okay. Good-bye. Well, that's that. The whore's dead. It'll be in the papers tomorrow. I'd better get a move on. Out of this crummy city, out of this country where the Izzies and the

58

Sammies get the fancy apartments and the rest of us get shit. Time to be going. Good-bye. Back to the land of my birth.

A man belongs where he was born. By boat. What a trip. Washing dishes all the way to France. What a man won't do. The main thing is to keep moving. A car, a car and still another car, a few trucks, and you're home in your beautiful new homeland. Wherever you look, black and red. Looks pretty nice somehow. And always something doing in town. A lot of things have changed, it's not like before. They're marching again, like in the Kaiser's day. It's nicer though. The people are sprucer. They used to be more elegant. Maybe because of all the counts. When you stand on the Heldenplatz, the people all come running. Raising their hands, I surrender. Sieg Heil! Heels high. You can look up their holes. Glum faces. The Führer fucks you front and back, he's from Linz. Sieg Heil, Sieg Heil. It's been a long time. A lot of things have changed since then. First came the war, and then the war was over. Then came the occupation troops, and now they're gone and we're back where we always were. On the rubbish heap. And no women. Only two dopes in the house. A pigsty. Nothing has changed. My cock is the same as ever, it hasn't got smaller. Only it's given up hoping for women. Sometimes he tries to stand up and make trouble, though he knows nothing will come of it. No, better not. Let bygones be bygones. It's been a long time. Here we are at Leo's. Behave yourself now, don't act up on me.

Wacholder had reached Leo's door. He could hardly breathe. He was very hot, panting and sweating. Leo was

What were you under Hitler anyway? A half-assed fellow sitting at the table, reading and holding his hands over his ears.

I shout myself hoarse, I suffer agonies, and you, you bum, you sleep. Wacholder shook Leo by the shoulder. He didn't look up. His eyes were in every letter, they changed with every line, every word. Now caressing, now disapproving, now angry, then again serene, and suddenly he laughed aloud, removed his hands from his ears and looked at Wacholder in astonishment. What's the matter with you, what's all the noise?

Are you deaf? Wacholder screamed, so excited that he had to hold himself fast. What's the matter with you? Are you dead?

I'm neither deaf nor dead. I'm in the middle of Being. Again?

Yes, I'm in the middle of Being. Any objection? And you stamp and yell as if somebody had burned you.

Burned? Me? Burned me? Yes, I've burned myself. Something just happened to me that I can't tell you about.

Oh, go ahead.

I felt something, something wanting to move in me. And suddenly I was back in Chicago, and then suddenly I was on the Heldenplatz and the women raised their legs and I was the Führer. Then all at once the sky was burning and all the atoms. It was good in a way, but it was painful too. There was fire, much bigger than Aslan's. Würz's little home is only a summerhouse compared to my castle. I'm a chosen man too. Providence has chosen me too.

Shut up, you old Nazi. Don't give me that hokum.

traveler, not even. You didn't know a damn thing about politics. You screwed too much in those days, and now you're impotent. That's the story of Wacholder, the whole story. The rest is imagination.

Wacholder was used to rough treatment from Leo, but this tone was new. Should I tell him the truth? The foundation of his existence was his supercock. Würz was enough. Two enemies would definitely be too much for him. There was only one way. To avoid a showdown.

Listen to me, Woodlouse (Wacholder put on his most solemn face). You can't talk to me like that. I can put you out in the street any time I please. You know that.

You? Me? Don't make me laugh.

Oh yes I can. And one more thing. I wasn't a half-assed fellow traveler. I was a very dangerous Nazi. Just to put you straight.

You? Leo spat. You a dangerous Nazi? If you'd been a dangerous Nazi, they'd have strung you up long ago.

Wacholder stamped his foot. I was though. I know, I didn't do anything, but that doesn't prove a thing. I wanted what happened to happen. Isn't that enough for you?

Leo laughed even louder than before. You're really a sap. If they started locking everybody up who wanted what happened to happen, they'd have to surround the whole country with barbed wire. No wall would be high enough. Stop bragging, it doesn't go down. Once upon a time you probably hurt a whore, even that isn't certain, in the days when you could still get it up, and she cried a little because it hurt. And that's all you ever did. You're a sentimental dog, that's all.

Now I suppose you're going to tell me you were the big Nazi? Steal my laurels, is that it?

Me? Leo grinned. I was too young anyway.

Then you're going to claim you're one now. Right?

Me? Those things don't interest me. Sit down, don't get so excited. We'll come to an understanding. Nazis have never existed. Agreed?

No, I don't agree. Who committed the crimes then? The whole people?

Not only ours, Wacholder. Every people. And not only peoples. What are peoples anyway? Every individual.

That's too highfalutin for me, too metaphysical. I'm only a simple man. I believe only in good and evil, in good men and bad men.

That's right, said Leo, you're a complete idiot. Don't let it worry you. Most people are. But it only becomes noticeable here in this dung heap.

I'll knock your teeth in if you talk to me like that, and I won't let you insult my people. We're a very old people, Leo, perhaps the oldest there is. We existed when nothing else existed, we had an emperor when nobody else had an emperor, and we had a republic when nobody else wanted a republic, we had Nazis when there were no Nazis and we had no Nazis when there were Nazis everywhere else. We had a liberation when everybody else was still occupied, and we got rid of our occupation because we turned neutral, when nowadays hardly anybody is neutral. We're better than everybody else, Leo, don't you know that? I'm telling you nicely, but I can get mean too.

Sure, sure, I know you inside out. Get sore if you feel like it. Next time we'll hang you. Satisfied?

Give me a butt. Wacholder sat down. (He's a man you can talk to.)

Now what do you want, old-timer?

The brain poison.

You'll have to see the poet next door. Here we think, we don't talk drivel.

What you won't think of next!

What do I think of?

That's what I'd like to know.

What will I get from you if I get Würz for you?

You'll never get him.

I'll get him, all right. I'm working on it. I'm not finished, but pretty nearly.

Working on what?

His Nonbeing.

What?

You heard me. I'm working on it. Leo stood up, tucked his shirttails into his pants and paced back and forth. He put on a look of pride and bored holes in the air with his right forefinger. That's it exactly.

What? How so?

Where will Würz be if we subtract him?

Gone.

Exactly. He'll be gone. You're not as dumb as you look. If we subtract him, he'll be gone; if we take away his existence, he won't have any existence. If something has no existence, it doesn't exist.

You're so clever. Würz isn't a speculation. He exists.

No, thank God, he's not a speculation. Leo had stopped pacing and stood facing Wacholder with his thumbs in his belt. The longer he looked at this Wacholder, the clearer it became to him. He's neither animal nor man, and he's not a machine either. A bush, a tree? A wood carving? His look was arrested by pink cheeks, a reddish nose, then down to the thick lips and up again. And suddenly he knew: what was sitting in front of him was only part of a man. A somewhat bent prick. That accounts for a number of things, Leo thought, and continued aloud: It's lucky he's not a speculation, because what doesn't exist can't disappear. No, Ossias Würz exists. At Melchiorstrasse 9. But . . . only so long as we maintain that he exists.

That's a fact, Leo. You're right.

And what follows? What follows is that if we maintain that he does not exist or do not maintain that he exists . . . he can't be, Wacholder completed the sentence.

Exactly. You discovered it.

Wacholder stammered: Why, that—that's revolutionary.

Yes, Wacholder, so it is. We take away his being by maintaining that he doesn't exist. Do you understand?

I understand, of course I understand. But can it be done? What is can't be gone.

Why not?

Well yes, if we want to use force.

No force. Or only the force of thought. He struck his forehead. That's the force that counts, Wacholder, the power of the spirit. With the help of the placental theory of existence.

Aren't you exaggerating a bit, Leo? There are only two spirits. The holy one and wine, as we Austrians say. There's never been another.

That's why he exists now. Because we mustn't use the other kind of force. You can threaten him and you can beg him on all fours, but you can't blow up his house. Not in this day and age. Nowadays it's all done with reason. Why?

On account of the police. You can do away with Würz by the power of reason and stop worrying about him by just refusing to recognize his existence. You won't even have to touch him.

That's revolutionary in the highest degree, Wacholder gasped. And when will we do it and how? Tomorrow morning? That's it, first thing in the morning.

A little patience. The problem hasn't been entirely solved, I haven't quite finished. Being can be Nonbeing, that's definite. But only if a majority agrees on it. A question of quantity. Quantity can reduce quality and ignore identity if, and that *if* is the crux of the whole matter, it's given a definite and exactly prescribed direction. It mustn't simply negate identity, because then the danger arises that it will also negate its own—no, it must be made to negate only a specific identity. That's the hard part. In short: the negation of Würz involves the danger of self-negation, because if what is can be declared to be nothing, so can the

65

man who does the declaring. In other words, if we say Würz doesn't exist, Würz can say: No one exists who can say that I don't exist. Then where would we be? Nowhere. That's the problem, and it's not only a problem for us, because of our language and so on, it's a problem all over the world. It's connected with insanity, but that's too complicated for you. For the present we'll just solve the problem.

Solve away, Wacholder cried with enthusiasm. How long will it take you? How long do you think?

I can't say. It may be days, it may be weeks. I won't make any promises. But I need peace and quiet. Quiet. No bellowing. No stamping and belching and no blubbering at night.

Hurry. Think deeper. Dig down. You'll find the solution. I'm sure you will. All I ask of you is to take care that you yourself don't vanish before you're done. You mustn't do that. Promise me.

8 The best thing about Leo was his nonsense. Most of the time, the sickness of his existence kept him horizontal under half-decayed blankets. He only stood up when lying grew painful. In his horizontal position, it sometimes seemed to him, he had invented thought. He was neither a doctor nor a philosopher, and called himself doctor of philosophy. Maybe that had something to do with it, in any case Leo was the real genius of the household. He thought only his placental theory of existence, nothing else. Wacholder and Aslan were useful companions. Wacholder because he paid for everything and took no money for the rent, Aslan because Leo was convinced that Aslan's book would be at least as nonsensical as his own, if not more so. In order not to hate him for that, he had undertaken to love him. In other words, he despised him. To avoid showing his contempt for Aslan, he also despised Wacholder, whom he despised anyway because for no reason he paid for everything and accepted no money for the rent. The result of these reflections was one day to be entitled *The Complete Metaphysic of the Noseo-genetic Theory of Existence*. That was still in the future. The remarkable thing about this theory was its twofold function. On the one hand, it gave him an occupation, it was a therapy; on the other, the work was so nonsensical he had every reason to assume that only the writing of nonsense is worthwhile, since, as everyone knows, sense can have no sense. And therefore, sense has none. Accordingly Leo, Dr. Leo Schön-Waldhaus, wrote his *Placental Theory of Existence* because he was imbued with its senselessness. He wrote it out of conviction. It began as a pseudoquestion with Spinozist propositions. It started out scientifically, perhaps to avert suspicion, and gradually became its own principle. The principle was termed: the rediscovery of sense without nonsense. The theory came in points:

(1) Existence is the result of the removal of the afterbirth. Hence the afterbirth is the origin of existence.

(2) Existence results from the absence of placenta vestiges, whose presence is therefore the premise and proof of existence.

(3) Without placenta there is no existence. It is therefore a necessity. If we are to posit the necessity of a proof before presupposing existence, we need only call it into question. The necessity of a proof of existence is then evident.

(4) The premise of the placental theory of existence exists, since it has had to be proved and has now been proved.

(5) What is this theory? As theory, it is the proof of existence. Its function is to prove itself through the proof of existence.

(6) Thus the function of existence is the function of the theory.

(7) We now know that existence and theory do not exist if we prove them. An unproved theory is an existence without necessity. An existence without theory does not exist (see 1), an unproved existence does not exist, and a proved theory can also not exist.

(8) Accordingly, theory exists only if it does not exist. Therefore, theory is negative thought—in other words, nonthought.

(9) The not-thought does not exist. Consequently, only one who cannot think can think the placental theory of existence. Hence it is pure nonsense.

(10) A placental theory of existence that is not pure nonsense does not exist.

(11) Hence the removal of the afterbirth is senseless. Better leave it alone.

(12) The afterbirth of the afterborn should therefore not be removed. In other words, it exists.

(13) It definitely exists.
(14) Afterbirth is existence.
(15) That is no accident.
(16) No.

The symptoms after such reflections were always the same. As soon as he stopped thinking his theory, existential pains set in, for when he was not thinking nonsense, he was bored. Becoming, Not-becoming and Not-having-become were as repugnant as Not-having-been and no more pleasant than Being. Therefore, and not, anyway, in the first place, said Leo to himself, I am a vexation. The fleas Kierkegaard and Nietzsche itched him on the right thigh, the fleas Spinoza and Kant (Leo had a long acquaintance with the cunning little blanket dwellers) itched the soles of his feet. All Western philosophy struck him as a skin disease. For this he did not hold the fleas responsible (and consequently left them unscathed), but his skin. The rash was only the form, his skin was the content. Language, he said to himself, is a loincloth. The more tattered and transparent the garment, the more ragged language is, the more clearly it reveals what is hidden. The disclosure of thought is the true function of language. Consequently, where the skin is concerned, not only ragged language but wrong thinking as well is in order.

Into these post-placental meditations, Aslan quite unexpectedly wormed his way. He blinked nervously. Leo, suppose the letter works and Würz comes over. What will we do then?

Don't worry, Aslan, said the old man, the fool belongs

to us because fools too belong to us. I'm against it, but he's right. He could clean out this pigpen, for instance. It's unbearable.

Why don't you go over to his place, if you don't like it here? Aslan was an early riser, he couldn't stand this neighbor who was always scratching himself. Aren't you ever going to get up?

No, I'm not in the mood. Lamb of my asshole, what I want is to lie down, but that's difficult right now. Listen to what I've just thought up: Würz is battling with Wacholder, while you and I get fat and older.

About the plague, Aslan, I've got to tell you about the plague. The plague is your better world, I don't know anything about it, all I know is that what interests you is the past, which is nonsense, my nonsense is the plague, which, as it happens, I call the placental theory of existence—in other words, ineradicable feeble-mindedness. Würz is right. He's right not to let us in, or Wacholder either, he's even crazier than the two of us. We're contagious, Aslan, because everybody knows that everything is senseless. Writing books too, but saying is never as clear as doing, the proof is in the pudding. Nobody is such a public menace as you and I. We go the whole way.

I'm not interested in stylistic experiments, my line is philosophical nonsense—that is, real nonsense—but I won't work. As long as Wacholder is stupid enough to let us live here for nothing.

You're ungrateful. It's a good thing Wacholder can't hear you.

Are you sure Wacholder's not your father, Aslan?

Yes, I'm sure, perfectly sure. My own father is some-place, I don't know where, but he's somebody. Compared to him, you with your speculations are a child. To him Being and Nonbeing are no problem. You can see that for yourself. Though he's not here, he exists. I advise you to do the same.

The allusion made Leo sad.

Yes, Aslan, sometimes I too think: What for? Why not tell the truth as I know it? Then it comes to me that I have nothing to say, neither a truth nor anything else. Doesn't that ever happen to you? Sometimes I think: Why not blurt it all out, simply and frankly? But the ques-tion is, what? That *what* is the hardest nut to crack. What strikes me as interesting doesn't interest me in the least, and the important things, important as they are, leave me cold. And then again my head is so full of unimportant things that I seriously doubt whether there'd be room in my brain for the important things if I had any. I just don't seem to have time for most things, important or unimpor-tant. Because most things are time-consuming in the first place and, in the second place, really unimportant. I rack my brains trying to think up something that's really im-portant, and I simply can't. And when I ask myself: Is there anything that hurts me, anything that concerns me? —nothing occurs to me. If, for instance, I dream of some-thing entrancingly beautiful, I can't describe it. The beau-tiful is so beautiful that no one must see it. I can see mine, and everyone can see his own. You see the beautiful best yourself. That's the placental aesthetic. It's universal. To wallow in your own afterbirth, to enjoy your own madness, is there anything more beautiful? Dream of something beautiful, Aslan, you can't have mine.

Leo had nothing more beautiful than this nonsense to offer.

9 Two days later Wacholder tiptoed in to Aslan for the brain shower.

Aslan, why don't you say something when I'm here? Been sleeping, eh?

Only dreaming, Father.

Must have been nice dreams. Give me a butt. Aslan gave him one but didn't get up. Let the old man light his own cigarette. Let him choke on it, for my money. With his screwy nerve lemonade. How can I get ahead with my own work around here? *The Better World* is lying around, gathering dust in my brain. My childhood doesn't even come to five pages, when it's good for fifty at least. The unimportant has priority, the essential must wait. That's how it is.

Leo is eliminating Würz, said Wacholder after the second draw, don't be jealous.

Leo is eliminating Würz, I said.

Aslan didn't react.

Eliminating him, I said.

Yes, Father.

He's not ready yet, but almost. When he's ready, we'll need a quantity. I assume, I hope at least, that he means people, who unanimously declare Würz to be a nonexistence. Result: the said Würz will cease to exist, after which he can do what he pleases.

That's a long way off, Father.

I don't say that it's not. But he's headed in the right direction. Would you have imagined that such a thing could be so simple?

Simple, Father? It certainly isn't simple.

No, it certainly isn't simple. Not the execution. But the idea, the inspiration is simple. What am I with my cod-liver oil by comparison?

So all of a sudden you've given up the lemonade?

No, of course I haven't given it up.

Don't get angry right away. Have you made some? How many containers have you made?

Two. The second in case he sends back the first.

That was clever of you. Go ahead and read. No, wait a second. Just think of it. Being is Nonbeing. Can you imagine that?

Of course I can. What does that amount to? Depends on who believes it.

That's what Leo says too.

On whether you believe it or not.

He says that too.

That's a problem.

He says that too.

It needs to be worked on.

That's what he's doing.

It needs to be solved.

He'll solve it. Definitely. Do you realize how clever he is?

How clever?

He's got the power of spirit, you've never seen the like of it. He's all spirit. Austrian spirit. German spirit too, if you like. In his opinion, violence is an absurdity. Nothing can be done by force, he says. Not any more. I respect that. The man's a genius, I tell you. Camouflages it all with nonsense, he's shrewd. Nobody notices it.

Yes, Father, Aslan said softly.

I get ideas too sometimes, Aslan, but nothing ever comes of them.

On account of your leprosy, Father.

Yes, Aslan, let's not talk about that. With me it's down below, with him it's up top.

Yes, yes, your leprosy. You've got to take your pills. They're bound to help you. One fine day, you'll see, it'll be gone. Someday it'll fall off. As the doctor says.

Yes, someday. Wacholder sighed. Someday Würz too will be gone.

He's a problem too.

Everything's a problem. Let's have the lemonade. It's late. I have to sleep. Go on and read.

Aslan began: Dear Würz, although dominant inclination might have permitted another step forward and the pertinent instrumental suggestion and advance of effective knowledge, it cannot be denied that not always before we take such a step, I, in this connection, ask someone who is

74

above all doubt to develop his theory superficially but
thoroughly and unintelligibly, especially to the scientist,
that what has actually happened and is universally known
simply cannot, that the contemplation and opportunity
for experiments have assumed enormous proportions in
connection with statistical truth, where concepts are not,
that in many cases blood-pressure readings and stool samples often no longer or even conversely produce deleterious
effects if the greatest danger is eliminated and really worthwhile ailments are cured by the incomprehension of the
psychiatrist. Therefore it is possible that everything nowadays and everybody who has trampled a doll and been hurt
knows nothing of it before and so long as he inclines to
such fears. An excellent illustration of this is the snake pit.
But as soon as semieducation allows itself to be impressed
by his character traits either as prognosis or loss of memory
too late and without symptoms or complaints unwarranted
fears and smears of an efficient thinking box with mass
psychosis, this is perhaps the place to reconsider suicide as
euthanasia because in the present age the associations of a
three-year-old child must really occur spontaneously.
Meant of course is the question of conscience and the corresponding repression of a fact which it is easily established and this we must bear in mind has indeed no other
purpose than to teach man that within the framework of
human society he more than animals for example is dependent on the help of others whose sexual symbols are
the root of sexual unfulfillment and in special cases a dor-
mant yearning for feeling and instinct the era of plush culture and mush vulture and the needs of self-awareness, the

outer circumstances and within the framework of the century's *mal de siècle*. Yours, Wacholder.

Excellent, said Wacholder, you've done that very nicely. Only perhaps you overdo it a little toward the end? All right, all right. If you say no, then no it is. Imagine if I received such a letter. It would drive me absolutely crazy. Sometimes I think a padded cell isn't the worst thing that can happen to you nowadays. It's nice and warm at Steinhof, you're taken care of, and it's nice and clean too. The doctors are nice and the nurses are helpful. You live like a pensioned colonel, you have no worries. Just because you're a little abnormal. It seems so simple. Some pleasant kind of lunacy is always attractive. If I didn't have this life mission of liberating Würz, believe me, I'd sometimes be tempted. Actually, but this in the strictest confidence, I might like to change places with him. And then I'd be over there in Melchior with the snazzy doll. And I'd have two sons out walking the streets for us, and I wouldn't have to go out into this loathsome city, I'd just do a little cleaning here and there, and I'd have time to think. There's no law against dreaming. And imagine, then Würz would be over here in this garbage can with you two degenerates. And Würz would be me sleeping in the paper. And he'd have insects at night and rats in his veins. And he'd be afraid his thing might stand up again and stage another blood bath. Do you know, honest to goodness, there are times when freedom doesn't appeal to me at all. All this democracy stuff is a hoax. This live-and-let-live routine, it's not for us. It's foreign, it's alien. Sooner or later we'll have to get rid of it. We're just too healthy for that kind of thing.

Sometimes I have this daydream: I see ice fields with nothing growing on them, no people either. That soothes me. In the last war we almost did it, and then in the end it didn't work out after all. In this world, Aslan, you're in luck if you lose your reason, because if you don't you go plumb crazy. Isn't that a healthy attitude?

Aslan was far away. These five or six pages had taken him ten years, and when he thought it over, there was nothing in them. Only the words marble, Erika, funeral, Wacholder, mother. That's how it should have been written. The ideal book has only a single word on each page. A ball-point pen comes with the book. The reader fills out the empty page himself. Literature ought to be abolished once and for all. Only, that would be too much work. And what would come of it in the end? Perhaps not even the five bad pages of a beginning.

The symptoms were there: two painful indurations of the right breast, an itching in the right eye, and at ten thirty, exactly two minutes before the arrival of the first sample of Wacholder juice, pus under the nail of his left forefinger. Würz pondered a long while about the "needs of self-awareness." The century's *mal de siècle* made him nervous. Mush vulture and plus culture were no laughing matters. The thing about the trampled doll was not to be ignored, and snake pit, suicide and sexual unfulfillment are words that have to be taken seriously. This time it was serious. That was clear to him. The matter must be settled in all haste, that too was plain, only it's too serious to be settled right now. He'd have to sleep on it. He got into bed with the letter, you couldn't leave such dynamite lying around. He put the letter between spring and mattress. He didn't want it too close to his head either.

The horsehair hadn't helped Würz. He saw himself in an extreme situation of authentic existence in which injustice blended into the expectation neurosis of a reaction pattern and the existential frustration of Franciscan Father T. Oberhammer unwound by a free decision of his inner mechanism. Shortly afterwards he found himself in a PW camp behind the lines and had bed phobia. What, actually, was I trying to think? ran through his head. Nothing? That's right. Nothing. Anxious anticipation made his figure into a chemical crutch, and his pressure-insomnia brought him to the regimental medical officer, who diagnosed no-doctors hysteria, which he felt to be right and just. A woman detached herself from a crowd and said: I have heart disease, and if you won't admit me you will be curtailing my field of value vision—in a word, the sexual anesthesia of my existential disillusion-ment. Würz's anticipation anxiety developed into gland-ular hyperfunction, and his excitement put him into the embarrassing situation of having to take a (scheduled) local train to a clinic, in which blasphemies in the form of people were thrown out of windows, although a gas cock was turned on before he even had time to wash his hands. He was afraid he would be obliged to enter a compulsion-neurosis room, and found affectivity and character changes on the operating table of a mania which drove him, via telehypnosis, to the dementia praecox of a Kurt Tucholsky, whom he did not know. These waves continued for the time of three attacks of rabies and ended in the catatonia of a dark watery surface. The private plane of an overloaded caisson disease was starting off as Würz demanded permission to carry out a mass murder in person without nonspecialists by means of a tube inserted in noses.

From this dream Würz awoke in terror at about six o'clock. Wacholder's brain poison hadn't entirely missed the mark. He hadn't felt so bad in a long time. Instead of watching the cat from No. 12, as he usually did at this time of day to make sure it was not armed, he hastily seized his fountain pen. His hand trembled, he bit his lips, and he made every effort to put order into his thoughts. You really frightened me, Wacholder, he wrote, at first I thought you were only joking, but on second reading, it was clear to me. Your letter has everything in it. It applies to me. You've hit the nail on the head and so on. And nevertheless I refuse. I have my honor, I have my self-respect, and I still have my reason. I will not let myself be coerced. You have showered me, you have hit me on the head with boards. It hurts. But I will persevere. I will stick to the post to which, beg pardon, God called me. Yours, Würz.

When Wacholder read this answer, he tore up fifty pounds of paper for joy. It's working, he shouted, and

danced up and down, it's working. He's on the defensive.
He's brought God into it. See what he writes: we have hit
the nail and so on. Here it is. I predicted it . . . He can't
stand up to my medicine. Let's give him the second bottle
right away, Aslan. He mustn't have time to recover. I'll
mail it at once. A postman is as good as a water-department employee. See. See. I'm a genius. Quick, read it.

Aslan read: For you my dear Würz comma I will empty
every bucket period. You have understood what it's all
about period. Now we are going to talk about politics this
is the last period. For our aim is the renewal of a literary
gift as boundless as it is aimless as uneven as your mental
capacities the adroit helpfulness of the momentary incon-
veniences of broad sections unmistakable resistance re-
gardless if the desires for homogeneity of views the task
of individuals in their mode of thought and existence with
the negotiations of a hostile alliance is obliged to make
concessions in which the appraisal of the situation not
only in the signature of broad sections of the old movement but also in the circular motion of ponderous members of an educational committee of notorious party members the glorious names which thanks to the power and
certainty and guided by the example of the government a
fruitful need for a liberated past ideological and political
certainties approached with a zeal for learning guaranteed
by the unfolding of the organization habitués of the Café
Kolosseum with firsthand reports of illegal associations
while on the other hand at the Café Tuschek spurred on
by an innovation mania the preparations for drafting
printing and disseminating his weekly revelations which

he shrewdly suppressed six months later, recommended by yours truly Wacholder.

After the second communication Würz trembled all over. He couldn't think and he couldn't work. Listlessly he sat in the cellar with a breakfastless stomach. By a great effort he had put on his work clothes and brought out brushes and paint pots, but it was no good. He peered into a bleak future compounded of hostile associations, homogeneity of views and notorious party members. Before his eyes the unfolding of an organization shimmered, ponderous listeners of an educational committee with innovation mania filed by and crept into illegal institutions. When Rita found him in the cellar at about seven that evening, his hands, neck, face and hair were painted white. Rita, it hurts, he whimpered, but he couldn't explain where the pains came from.

Rita made Ossias a turpentine bath and had to undress and scrub him, he rubbed paint into his eyes and screamed when it hurt.

Half an hour later Ossias left the bathroom, disgruntled but not clean. That's a friend, Rita, Würz moaned, and gripped his pen.

At first I admit, Wacholder, you confused me a little. The words power, certainty and organization in your mouth, who would have thought it, but then came the cafés, and I knew where I was at. Now it is all clear to me. Clearer than ever before. Your letter has not had the desired effect on me. I know what I want. I want man in the negativized area of his present constitution with the feelings of a human human in the esoteric salon of intellectual conversations on the childbed of the immutable non-man inclining it is to be hoped to a fate and to the power of the inhuman nonhuman, the morality, culture and artistic interest of the religion of the citizen who confronted by the military constitutional state only the dashing of hopes and sustaining a regime of blood and violence developing a humanity of his own into the thwarted object lesson of such failure and dissolving his impotence into the striving for a better world and a more human future. That is what I want. I think I have made myself clear? Yours, Würz.

10 Clear as day. Wacholder was beside himself for joy. See! The second bottle was twice as good as the first. His answer is completely incoherent. He's stammering. He's drooling. This is a great historical event. The nerve foam has conquered. Congratulate me.

Aslan gave Wacholder a cool, feeble hand. Congratulations, Father. Leo clutched Wacholder's right hand as if to pump the last drop of madness out of him. Friends, Wacholder cried, beaming, we have won. Taking a short run, he dashed into a pile of loose paper. When he emerged, he said solemnly: By words! By the correct use of our language. This is a glorious country. It wouldn't have been possible in any other country. This is one more proof. The heritage of our forefathers! Long live German-Austrian culture! Tomorrow morning we'll call for him. He has capitulated.

I can hear his steps, I can see him. He's breathing our free air—in Custom House No. 8. We're united again!

I'll go for the doctor, Father, said Aslan.

Wait, cried Leo, I'll go with you. He'll be dangerous tonight.

And that night of all nights Böckling came, for she liked best to inspect when no one was counting on it. When you were sleeping, sitting drunk in a chair, counting your own fingers, when you were lying in the bathtub or in bed with a girl friend. In case you were standing in the urinal, bringing up coal from the cellar, getting ready to cut your toenails, to fry eggs, to explain a toy to a child, you could reckon with Böckling. She came in a soundless Chevrolet with a briefcase, and even without her documents she knew every single case by heart. The main part of her job was to punish slovenliness and crookedness. She came in the name of a higher authority. She spoke for the government, for the state. She knew no personal feelings, she implemented those of her employers. A man who makes his bed in a government-owned pile of paper, who folds government property into bags, who tears government property for his amusement, who generously gives it away or throws it into mud puddles, is sure, sooner or later, to be overtaken by Böckling, who, if she does not destroy him, will at least attempt by a last warning to bring him back to the straight and narrow.

Of course Wacholder was not reckoning with her. It is only too human to bury your conscience as a dog buries a bone. But nothing escapes the vigilant eyes of the supreme ruler. Never. God sends His angel. The state sends its Böckling.

She came with stamps and stamp pads and went to work immediately. Every sheet of paper was palped, counted and stamped. This checkup was long overdue. In her work suit (striped trousers, vest, boiled shirt and top hat) she climbed up and down the heaps and bales, circumnavigating the sleeping Wacholder as best she could, and by about four o'clock she was done. Although she had adroitly managed to count even the paper under Wacholder, she was obliged to awaken the old man, for Wacholder was holding down the last sheets of paper with a heavy weight. She had to lift it, there was no other way.

Sensitive in this spot even when asleep, Wacholder came wide-awake. Is it you? he cried.

Yes, I know, it's me, she said.

But is it really you?

Yes, it's definitely me.

Are you the minister?

I am Böckling, was the answer.

Come to inspect?

To check, Mr. Custom House Director, to see whether your paper is in order?

I'm not dreaming, Trude?

No, Wacholder. It was to be expected.

I wasn't reckoning with you. Or actually, I was. But not so soon.

We know that. Nobody reckons with me, but they expect me all the same.

Is anything missing?

340,722 sheets.

As much as that?

Exactly. What are we going to do about it, my friend?

Ah yes, what are we going to do about it?

That's for you to know.

I'm sorry. I used a little for domestic purposes, but only now and then.

340,722 sheets for domestic purposes? That's a lot, my good friend. A lot.

I admit it. But if you think it over—

Everything can be thought over, thought out, thought in, thought away . . . but not by me. This is official business. This is government property. The state. Do you understand? Responsibility. You are responsible. This is your signature. Or isn't it your signature?

It's my signature, Wacholder admitted.

Then it's a case of embezzlement. Embezzlement is a punishable offense.

I haven't embezzled anything. The paper, the paper . . . it disappeared all by itself.

340,722 sheets have disappeared all by themselves. Who's going to believe that?

Nobody, you're right. What am I going to do now?

Yes, little friend, what are you going to do now? There's something wrong with you. You're not all there. You're sloppy. This is a pigsty. It's no wonder. You never think of cleaning up, of making order. You wouldn't even dream of it.

No, that's not true. Only a few minutes ago I was dreaming about it. Tomorrow, I dream, I'm going to flush out the whole mess. And put everything in order.

You can tell that to your Aunt Jenny. Not to me.

Then what will I do? I'm perplexed again.

What will you do? You'll have to pay up.

Pay up? Me? Where will I get the money? People are always wanting money from me. They never leave me in peace. Pay, Wacholder, you've got to pay. That's how it always is around here. Day and night. Even at night they leave me no peace, pay, Wacholder, pay.

Don't talk so much. People without money should watch their step.

What's going to become of me?

Can't you think of anything?

No. I haven't any money. I'm only a poor devil.

Give me another signature. Sign here, 340,722 sheets missing. Okay, a commission will attend to the rest.

No, no commission. Please no commission. I've had so many commissions in my life. Always coming around. Needling me, asking questions. It makes no difference what you say, the bigwigs are always right.

I know, but what do you expect of me? You want me to overlook the whole thing? The shortage is too glaring to be overlooked. Anyway, take that stone away, I've still got to stamp those papers.

That's no stone, Frau Doktor, Your Excellency, that's me.

Don't brag, Wacholder. They don't come like that. It's a stone, lift it. Or have you hidden something under it? Lift it, I say.

Lift it yourself.

I've tried, it's too heavy for a woman. I'll try again.

Böckling stood legs outspread over Wacholder, bent down and lifted it as if it had been a feather. She knew it wasn't a stone, but a lady doesn't do such things without an invitation. She weighed it in her hand.

That's a nice little piece.

It's all mine. You want it? Try and see if it suits you.

Give it here, but no obligation, see.

Wacholder braced himself on both hands. He couldn't see her face. Only a silhouette.

The way you take me in, he wanted to sigh aloud, the last time . . . he wanted to scream. He couldn't make it. The most Trude gave him a chance to do was grunt.

No, it can't be, it's not possible, Wacholder pleaded soundlessly. It's disappeared and she isn't hurt. No screams, no howls. It just slips back and forth, forth and back, without a sound.

He could hear the dew dropping on the tin roof. And the water outside. He had never heard it so loud. Was it already at the door? Had the river overflowed the dam, were the fields under water? Wasn't the water coming through the door, climbing the paper mountain, weren't his feet wet? It's the deluge, that's what it is, the world is going under and you don't hear it until it's all perfectly still. Wacholder had been drowned for ages in still, dark

87

wetness. From up above, from the surface of the water came a familiar voice: Well, my boy, that was lovely.

You're joking.

Joking? Where's the joke.

Trude, are you still alive?

Of course I'm alive.

Haven't I killed you?

Killed me? What with?

Right now. With this thing.

Kill a Trude Böckling with a little fellow like that? Don't be silly.

Aren't you a whore?

A whore? I'm the Minister of Commerce and Reconstruction.

But symbolic? Is that it? You're symbolic, aren't you?

Me? Symbolic? I'm a woman, my little customs inspector, a perfectly normal woman.

Aren't you in Chicago?

What would I be doing in Chicago? I'm right here with you in the paper.

Wacholder looked down again. Now there was color. Red lips and shining blue eyes. Dark hair moved.

Wacholder repeated, now slowly and more sadly: You're not in Chicago and not dead. You're the minister, and everything is okay. That's amazing.

Everything isn't okay, Wacholder, we still have those 340,722 sheets to attend to. Even if we are intimate, I can't neglect my duty. That's the way the government is. Friendly but heartless. But because I feel sorry for you and

88

you yourself have nothing, I'll make good the loss out of
my own pocket.

Wacholder stroked her forehead tenderly. Out of your
own pocket, that's sweet of you.

The Chevrolet was ready to go. This engine was reality,
and this woman under him. I'm fucking a Böckling, that
means I'm in the ministry, Wacholder inferred quite
soundly. It's an ordinary Saturday, there's nothing symbolic about that either. I'm not dreaming all this, I'm
really in the government. My past doesn't count. It's taken
twenty-five years. But everything comes in time.

Trude, Wacholder whispered, do you feel something?

Trude was asleep. What is it? What do you want?

Not the same man, Trude, I'm not the same man. I'll
have to move out of here. I don't want to live here any
more. I'm moving into town.

Let's not exaggerate right away, Wacholder, let's not
do everything at once. Think it over.

I've got to get away. Away. I've got to. I'll go and stay
with my friend Würz, he'll let me in now.

You're only dreaming that, old man. It seems that way
to you now. It doesn't go so fast. Stay here for the present.
I'll come and see you often.

She stood up, began collecting her clothes. It wasn't
easy in this trash heap. Here a stocking, over there a shoe,
the striped trousers were fifteen feet away. As she was
crawling over to the trousers, a voice from above struck her.
On the gallery stood two men. A little square one with a
black beard and a thin, scrawny pale one with a bald head.

When the two of them had come home toward morning and found the sleeping chauffeur in the official Chevrolet with TB 1 on its plates, they knew: this visit will pay off.

I need six shirts, two pairs of shoes and an overcoat, Leo called. Trude looked up, felt the cold on her bare behind and realized her situation.

Yes, Aslan cried, we're still here.

Go to hell, Wacholder shouted. What do you want?

And while you're at it, said Aslan, when you send the duds, give the driver a few schillings for me. I'm out of funds at the moment. Let's say ten thousand.

And another ten thousand for me, said Leo.

And I need some clothes too, Aslan interrupted. Another six shirts and two pairs of shoes, I don't wear an overcoat, but I could use a suit. Something in a light color.

Trude Böckling felt that in this night something had happened that would have its consequences. What difference does it make? she thought. This Wacholder is a real man. He's worth a little trouble. Wacholder gazed with glassy eyes at the "two bums up there." Haven't you anything to say? Trude snapped at him.

Me, what would I say, what is there to be said? Give them what they want, you can see the situation for yourself, your bare behind is . . . well, it's bare. I won't blackmail you, not I. It wouldn't do me any good to get you fired. On the contrary.

I love you. Trude bent over Wacholder and kissed his sleepy eyes.

Okay, okay, Wacholder dismissed her.

She found her top hat, found her gloves and patent-leather shoes and buttoned her fly. She left without saying good-bye.

The chauffeur opened the door, handed his boss the morning paper, the car drove off. Aslan and Leo stood at the window and waved.

11 Whether because of Wacholder's assault or not, Würz began to make different preparations for his seventeenth anniversary. He put an open, empty tin can in the room (there had once been chocolate cookies in it) and lay in wait. To arouse no suspicion, he crept slowly closer on his knees and elbows. When he thought the can was full, he quickly put the lid on and set an ear to one of the edges. That air is invisible is its own business. It was nevertheless a reality. Like every reality it was out for Würz's life. Atom, proton, electron. He recognized each molecule, even in the most harmless disguise, as a beast of prey. In packs and swarms they were absolutely unconquerable. Their invisibility was camouflage, that was plain to him. No atom was going to come up and say: Here I am, kill me. That was not to be expected, and besides he had no desire to kill them, he only wanted to surprise their secret and then clean them. All sorts of things were going on in the house, and the little things get around. They get

into in Arnulf's ears, Arnold's mouth, Rita's eyes. They're
bound to have quite a few stories to tell. But if they refuse
to talk—he'd give them a double dose of camphor and turpentine. There might be a few casualties. That was the
danger of atomic warfare. Even Saint Francis took a long
time to understand animals, and how easy they are to
understand in comparison with atoms and suchlike. I'll
just have to be patient. Animals make audible sounds, but
sounds we already know. They suggest something that's
already known, they remind you of the repressed smacking
and chirping, cackling and barking that you carry about
inside yourself. But to understand the secret eloquence of
silent things, things that make less noise than your own
blood, that go about more soundlessly than thought, is
naturally very difficult. Yes, to know what you can't know
is difficult, perhaps at the moment his life depended on it.
Patience, patience, he admonished himself, and had none.
Tomorrow was the day, it was too late to change that. Tomorrow it would happen, doubt was no longer possible.
Tomorrow, at my seventeenth anniversary celebration,
they will . . . No, never. I've made my preparations, my
eyes and ears are everywhere. The secret is in the air, in
the atoms, I've got a few hundred thousand of them in
this box, sooner or later they'll have to speak up.

It smells of sweet chocolate—that means murder by
strangling. Or isn't it sweet chocolate? The smell was unmistakable. The more distinctly he smelled it, perhaps just
because he smelled it so distinctly, the less willing he was
to rely on it. He went to the kitchen and opened several
tins—coffee, tea, flour and spices. He opened cans of vege-

tables, meat, fruit salad, and found the same smell in none of them. That was proof enough. Death by strangulation. He crawled back on all fours and knelt again beside the tin, the smell was plainer than ever before. That cloying breeze from the Far East. Here was death lurking in a tin can, acting as innocent as you please. He thought he heard something, it sounded like voices behind a closed door, but the voices were so far away that he couldn't understand a word. Louder, he cried out, louder, I can't hear a thing. He held his breath, and when he thought his lungs were going to burst, he heard a voice something like Rita's: Soon now, after the party, when he's tired, when he goes upstairs . . .

Louder, louder, Würz whispered. He waited thirty seconds, but there was nothing more. He took off the lid and shot three full charges of camphor and turpentine into the mysterious hole. He turned the tin upside down, shook out the last dead atom and lay down on the floor again. Again they came in swarms, packs and herds, they came by the hundreds of thousands and filled the empty tin. A few minutes later, convinced that not one more proton could get in, he put on the lid. That does it, Würz said to himself. You can't see me, but I can hear you, even if you talk on your tiptoes.

Suddenly Arnold's bass came to him clearly: When he turns around, Arnulf, you give it to him from behind. When he turns around, Würz repeated to himself, yes, *when* he turns around, but he won't turn around. God has not forsaken me. That sentence gave him an uneasy feeling. Too much hope and not enough certainty. If you leave out the *not*, the sentence goes: God has forsaken me.

93

All right, God has forsaken me. Here I stand, all alone, even God has forsaken me, and now Arnold is waiting for me to turn around. But I won't turn around, I'll stay here with my back to the wall. What then? What can you do to me then? If I keep my back against the wall, you can't do a thing to me. Or can you? Maybe that mutton-head will think up something. Are you going to jump at my face, at my eyes? Blind me? Würz set his ear to the lid, he felt almost foolhardy. And immediately he heard Arnold's crackling voice: Not the eyes. The nose and the teeth. We'll stick it in his mouth.

What? Würz shouted. What are you going to stick in my mouth? You bum, you crook, you loafer. What are you going to do to me? Go on, out with it . . .

The tin was silent. Quickly he removed the lid, pumped ten charges (because they wouldn't talk!) of camphor mixture into it and threw the corpses into the trash basket. He had an idea. Holding the open tin, he crawled toward the door. Now he was out for the atoms that fell fresh from the keyhole and the ones that pushed with all their might through the cracks in the door. Young and unsuspecting, they poured in, full of important news. He touched the tin with the back of his head. The contact between head and tin ought to be enough.

A second inspiration: My hairs are antennae on my rounded roof. My brain is a laboratory. Scientists in white are performing experiments unknown to me. My eyes are double windows, closed so the scientists won't be distracted, my nose is the flue through which the poisonous gases escape from the retort. In my nose lives a fungus

94

named soot. In my nose there are black fungi. Nasal fungi.
The instruments and materials are stored up in my cheeks,
they are the storeroom. It's drizzling on my palate. That
too is an experiment. My tongue is a ship. This is its home
port. My throat is a canal on the sea route to Africa. I'm
full of countries. Their names are: kidneys, spleen, liver,
heart, lungs. It's the rainy season in my heart too. Heavy
drops are beating down. In the other countries it's dry and
nothing is happening. They're waiting. My stomach is a
river in the jungle, hot, muddy, poisoned with insects and
crocodiles and little fishes with sharp teeth. My bladder is
the beginning. The source. Outside, a sleeping bird sits
wearily in his nest. Clever bird, he's built his nest between
my legs. My arms are the last bastions of a fortress, my
fingers are tourists, they move up and down or cower, exhausted, in the heat of my continent. The name of this
swampy, uninhabitable, Godforsaken continent is Ossias
Würz. He's rotting away in the mud, in the stagnant
water. Up on the highest peak stands my scientific insti-
tute, measuring me. Let them come with their compasses
and forceps and glass tubes and tweezers, I'll escape into
the woods, they won't find me here. Let them come. I'm
not afraid, I fear no man. For nothing human is alien to
me. The dog and the cat are alien to me. Unicorn and
camel are alien to me. Squirrel and deer are alien to me.
Arnold is a pig, and his brother, Arnulf, is a pig, and Rita,
the cat, is the mother of pigs. The house is a stable, a dung
heap, a gutter, a sewer, a slop jar, a Roman bath, a Catholic cloister, a bath and a cloister, and it stinks and it's fallen into ruins. That's why I have to keep the place clean

and repaint every square centimeter and paint every hair on my brush and wash the paint off every hair, for paint too is dirt and glue, wash it off with kerosene, no, with gasoline and turpentine, soak everything in gasoline and set fire to it. That's right, set fire to it and burn it till nothing's left, not even ashes. Burn the ashes, pour them out. Cover them with earth. Earth is dirty. Make a hole, blast the ground. Blow it away. Boom, and the earth is blown away. The world is gone, blown into dust powder, it falls into space. Help! The existent is a dirty existent. Everything that is is dirty. Only what is not is clean. Nothingness, even nothingness is dirty. My house is something and nothing, both are full of filth. Is filth clean, can dirt be clean? Impossible, impossible. Dirt is. Dirt is dirt. My fate. Dirt is my fate. My fate is dirty, and that's why they have to destroy me, now, immediately and right away.

Suddenly voices came from the next room, loud and clear, they didn't come through the tin can, they came through the wall: My friend is a high school teacher, that's what he is.

Bunk! Informer! Hartl isn't even a substitute teacher. He's the janitor.

That's not true. It's a damn lie. And I saw you with a policeman yesterday.

I was asking the way, you sap.

Sure, sure. So he takes you by the hand and guides you. Expect me to believe that?

Can I help it? He just happened to be friendly.

They don't make that kind of cops in this town. His kind come in droves.

They must be talking a secret language, Würz thought, but decided to intervene all the same. He stood up, joined the two of them in the kitchen and said gently: Don't fight, boys. I'm not asking who it is, I don't want to know. We don't give our children advice, we're sensible parents. We don't get out of the house, and it wouldn't do to accept homework. It's a big house, it needs your mother and myself. If the place isn't kept in order, everything goes haywire. I don't give you advice the way stupid parents do. Children should do what they please as long as it's right and reasonable. I've thought a good deal about children and education. When you're older, you'll thank me. We men have to be rough and hard. That's the way we are. We can't change it. And now beat it, and no back talk.

Arnold raised his eyebrows. Arnold's pupils sparkled. What do you want of me? Würz screamed.

The immediate consequence of this new agitation was a cold in the roots of his hair, or so at least it seemed to him. His scalp burned. There was also a mysterious pain in his right foot, something absolutely new to him; it moved up through his body and decided in favor of his pleura. It didn't stop there for long. It moved toward his lungs, squeezed his breathing tubes.

It was only a matter of seconds before the pain reached the heart. That will be the end.

Rita led him to his bed and undressed him.

They're gangsters, Würz gasped. They're criminals.

Rita brought in a tin of cookies. Less affectionately than usual, Würz noted. Of course, it's a plot. I'll take a cookie so as not to arouse suspicion.

Thank you, said Würz, one is enough. I've seen through you, you scum, but—he didn't say—I won't show it. This was the crisis. There are crises. This was the crisis. I'm having a crisis. I can feel it. I'm crising all over. Especially in my heart something is crising. The end is coming. Or it's not coming. He took the medical dictionary from the bedside table. (It replaced the family doctor. Doctors? No. Those are the real germ carriers.) He leafed for a moment and finally found what he had often read and could not read often enough.

CHAPTER XIV
DEATH

. . . the extreme sensitiveness of the nerve cells in the brain accounts for the fact that in most fatal diseases, shortly before death at least, the function of the ganglion cells which regulate the circulation and respiration, and on whose intactness the preservation of consciousness depends, are impaired by modifications of the body fluids. We may therefore assume that in the majority of cases, the ultimate inner [!] cause of death is to be sought in a failure of the ganglion cells, often accompanied by unconsciousness. The onset of death is recognized by the signs of death.

He had recognized the signs. He would have to arm for the final, the ultimate battle. Flight was out of the question. He jumped out of bed. There was only one last possibility. Camouflage. Do like the atoms and quickly.

With the help of Rita's hair drier, he was ready in two hours to display his invisibility. He went back to his room.

In the hallway he was not seen, because no one was there. That was a good omen. Will I recognize myself at the next confrontation? Doubtful, very doubtful, Ossias Würz. Only what you see in the mirror, the Gypsy said, she didn't say anything about its still being him even if it isn't. The first test was Rita (a precipitated self-confrontation didn't seem wise). Five short and five long notes on the recorder. Rita came in. I thought you were sick, Ossias (she came toward him), and here you are, sitting at the table, playing the flute.

Stop, Würz cried. Whom are you talking to? May I ask?

To you, Ossias.

Not to me. Or perhaps you are. So you recognize me? I almost didn't, Ossias.

It's first-class paint, and crumbling already. Is that it? Why these theatricals, Ossias?

It's not theatricals. It's life in earnest.

If you want theatricals, I'll give you theatricals.

Funny you should say theatricals. Have you started poking your nose into my dreams now? Because I've been dreaming theater. Only last night I was on the stage again. I had to wait for the audience to quiet down. Then I crossed the stage and disappeared through a door on the left. Applause. Scene Two. I enter from the same door and bow. A storm of applause. My monologue. My monologue's gone. Fallen into the audience, somebody's stolen it. It's gone. I couldn't say a thing. I look at the audience, they look at me. Their mouths are closed, their monologue is on the tips of their tongues, they're waiting for mine that's disappeared. All of a sudden, people come up behind me, the stage is full of actors. Embarrassed silence in the house. My monologue is still missing, I utter a crazy little laugh. The whole house laughs, I laugh louder, I laugh so long and loud that they're all moaning with laughter. Then I turn serious, cold and disapproving, but they go right on laughing, they think it's part of the joke, but now I'm really in earnest. What is there to laugh about? What is there to laugh about in general? This is a serious, uncomfortable, cold world. I shiver. Everybody down there in the audience feels the cold. The doors are all open. January. Wolves and snow. Snow on all sides and no firewood. A few dance steps to warm myself. Feet start moving in the first row. Music. Somebody's dancing behind me. Louder and faster. Cries. I scream and rage. Behind me screaming and yelling. A roaring, a neighing, a bleating and laughter. Who's laughing? My nerves. Some of the people start leaving. Others are still hesitating, waiting for the show to go on, still shouting and cheering. I draw my revolver, and the actors have machine guns. They step up to the footlights. They aim their weapons at the audience. The house is in an uproar. A shot. A light bulb bursts with a loud report. It's high time. People running. The doormen close the doors. The show's over, and good night! The actors go to their dressing rooms to change, then they go home. Alone at last. The stage, the whole theater is mine. All mine. Now I can do what I please. Speak or not speak, smoke or sleep. I can dance, jump, run around in a circle, turn somersaults. They're all gone. My monologue even comes back to me.

I speak for an hour, maybe longer, in the end I ring down the curtain, no sooner has it fallen than I pull it up again. Act Two. Other people are speaking. All at once. Voices, voices. Things happen. Things besiege me. I move further and further back. I disappear. I ring down the curtain. I clap. Intermission. I pace restlessly back and forth. Anxiety. Last act. The empty house is hanging on my lips. Encore. But only this once. My last feat: I climb up to the top gallery and shout, The air I eat doesn't kill, I spread out my arms, I sail through the empty house. The end is nausea.

So if it's theater you want, Rita, leave it to me. Rita sat at the table, her chin propped in her right hand.

No, Rita, this is a military ruse. Camouflage. So they won't recognize me.

Who?

Those two. Who else? If they strike now, they'll miss me. Or maybe not. You recognize me. Did you recognize me on purpose or by accident?

Right away, Ossias.

Right away is no accident. It was on purpose. You wanted to recognize me. I make myself unrecognizable, but you wanted to recognize me. On purpose.

Wash off the paint, Ossias, maybe it's the paint. You were never like this before. First wash off the paint.

No. I'm threatened. Something is threatening me.

They're threatening me with threats. Everybody's threatening me, including myself. I'm threatening myself. I'm one
of them myself. I just happen to know. Ha, you'd like to
know how I know. Never mind. They won't find me, Rita.
Not me. I've got to restore myself. Let me down (Rita
was blocking the way). I prefer to restore myself in private.

My nerves, Ossias.

Your nerves? And what about my nerves? My nerves
are nerves too.

If I went away, Ossias, what would you do?

If you went away, I don't know, but you won't go
away. Do you want to live in an apartment, a plain apartment in some street? This is a house. Do you want to live
with other people you meet on the stairs every day with
their germs and no handkerchief over their mouths? Their
coughing, would you live through it?

If I went away, Ossias, yes.

But you won't go away. Do you want to sit behind
ordinary windows without a ventilating system and wait
till you get sick, and go looking for a doctor through noisy
streets without wax in your ears, and breathe in his germs?
Is that what you want?

No, said Rita in terror.

Do you want to try to keep a house clean with soap
and water and no paint or turpentine or chlorine or
glycerin or spirits or camphor?

Yes, Rita gasped.

And have I painted for the last seventeen years to hear
that it's all the same to you, have I wasted the best years
of my life to promote your lunacy?

My lunacy, Ossias? Have I a lunacy?

Have I worked like a fool for seventeen years, have the seventeen years been for nothing? Haven't I been a husband to my wife, a father to the children? Have I been a husband or haven't I, have I been a father or not? A non-father can also be a father, I've proved it.

You wanted to give them a father. You succeeded. My health is ruined, the turpentine has wrecked my lungs. These hands are the hands of an old man. I'm finished. All for your sons. Built a house, erected a monument. Now they're grown up they don't need me, they don't need my house. They'll go, and you'll go with them. Leave me to rot away all alone, to feed myself, take care of myself. To work, keep order, watch the street, burn the dust and live all alone like an animal in a hole. Pacing up and down. Sleeping without peace. Dreaming without sleep. Thinking black thoughts. Never exchanging a word with a human being. A solitary animal. That's what you want. That's what you want.

I admit it, I have dreams myself. About going away. About moving around. And sitting around. Cafés, for instance. Idling on café terraces. Going to department stores. Looking at things. Wanting to touch them. Why yes, even a . . . movie show. Imagine, me at the movies. And I dream about the theater too, crowded with people. A huge crowd in the lobby. Sweet-smelling faces. Women. Fine clothes. Going out for dinner. To a crowded restaurant. Crammed in together. We eat. Shellfish and meat in fragrant sauces. Sour things to drink. Sweet fruits— crowded together like dogs in the pound, with upraised paws, stuffing food into our mouths, grunting, licking our lips and the lips of other female dogs—that's what I dream —until sweet terror suffocates me.

And suppose I went away, Rita screamed, suppose I went away. She screamed and spat, a tiger, a devil, the Devil herself bit his hand.

I'm bleeding to death, Rita, it's a shame, I'm bleeding to death.

Rita wept. Würz wasn't bleeding to death. He looked at his hand, turned it in all directions. That's a bite on my hand. My hand has just been bitten. This white camouflaged hand has been attacked and bitten. Something has bitten you here, Ossias, what has bitten you? I didn't do it, Würz noted. That leaves the rest of those present. In other words, Rita. Rita doesn't bite hands, she's never bitten a hand. So it wasn't Rita. Since it wasn't either of us, there's only one last possibility. An animal. A cat. A cat came out of the wall, smelled my hand, took it for a fish head and bit it. Würz sniffed at his hand. No, it doesn't smell of fish. Maybe a dried fish, anyway there was once an eye here. The cat bit it out. A cat? In my house. Biting the light out of my hand. Strange, Rita, very strange. You're crying.

I feel sorry for the poor Mother of God, Rita wailed. I too am the virgin of a tortured child. I have two on the cross. Pierced with pointed sticks. Vile men laying hands on—

They always do, Rita, Würz cried, they always do. Say your prayer, the one about the Father and His Son. That will help you. You didn't notice the cat that was just in the room, pray for your eyes, Rita, and pray for my eye, it's gone.

Rita kneeled. Würz stood, white and pious, beside her and laid a hand on her hair to bless her.

In the clothes cupboard, under the sweaters, lay the saints. Six color plates from the *Catholic Illustrated Weekly*. She laid them on the bed one by one (Jesus and His mother were also among them). The saints were silent. It was comfortable for them on the bed.

You've been dead so long that nothing more can touch you.

She went into the kitchen, came back with salt, strewed salt into the saints' eyes. It didn't help. Salt didn't trouble them. They smiled blissfully, proudly, mercifully, treacherously and maliciously. Should I give you honey? Have you deserved it? Rita went to the kitchen, came back with a bottle of vinegar, poured it into the eyes first of the saints, then of Jesus and finally of Mary. That ought to hurt. And indeed they screwed up their faces and crumpled, but remained silent.

In that case, Rita cried, when three minutes had passed and there was still no answer, there's only one more thing to do. She took the pictures to the kitchen, filled a basin with hot water and plunged the pictures into it. When the saints had broken up into shreds, she strained the water into a stone jug and put the jug in the icebox. For emergencies.

Exactly, crying three times exactly, Würz ran upstairs and down with empty bottles, boxes, tins and canisters, cook pots and frying pans. He distributed them through all the rooms. He left them standing open, ten minutes, fifteen minutes, then he put on a white gas mask. Into each open receptacle he squirted as much insecticide as would go in, then he put on the lid.

Rita, I'm struggling, Würz screamed. I'm buggling and struggling. I'm uggling. My struggling is bigger than the ferris wheel and will live after me. I'm the muggliest struggler in the world. Nobody struggles as I do, Rita, where are you? Show yourself, don't be afraid. It's all going much too slowly. It's got to go faster. The end must come soon, when will it come, Rita? At table, Rita? They like best to murder at tables. The whole lot of them. Wacholder's slaked lime almost dissolved me, I ignored it. Now Wacholder too is afraid of me. He's stopped trying, he's given up. Capitulated, Rita. He's afraid of my ego. Sometimes I'm afraid of it myself. I'm glad I don't know where I am. You recognize me, but I don't recognize myself. I'm not the same man, and that's why I'm glad I don't know who I am.

Wash yourself, Ossias, she begged him. Please wash yourself before you go to the table. You hurt my eyes.

Only your eyes, Rita? I knew it. Only your eyes are

sorry for me. You shouldn't be sorry for me at all. You should be sorry for those people outside, who live in coffins, waiting for somebody to come and hide them from the air. As for me, I can't die. I simply can't. I have eternal life. Just let them come. They won't find me. I'll hide in my own reason.

And to keep them from ever finding me, I'll lose it.

12 Up and down, in and out, a rubbing and scraping of everybody with everybody simultaneously and from all sides, an inland lake of sweat and sperm, a perfumed grinding, an orgy of too-muchness. Fist-thick and finger-thin, hand-broad and knee-high. A shuffling, a groaning, a flashing of teeth, laughter and giggling, a backdrop of noise.

Leo loudly thwacked the first naked behind that knelt before him. A scream, a whimper, then sudden silence. The conferees crawled on all fours, rolled against the walls in frantic embrace and tried their best to hide behind the scant furniture.

Short and thickset, in a dark suit, Leo the Inquisitor stood high above the naked assemblage, looking from one pair of eyes to the next, as if to scrutinize one last time the consciences of those condemned to die by fire. Wherever he looked, spent eyes, weary lips, as though each one of them had made his peace with his death and were merely waiting for the fire. Wearing a light summer suit, Aslan stood there with folded arms, prepared to execute every one of Leo's or Wacholder's commands. If Leo had cried Fire, Aslan would have kindled every single one of those present with his lighter. Aslan was first to reach the window; Wacholder had helped him. The windows were closed. The last hint of fresh air was gone. The conferees sighed in chorus; even with the windows open the heat had been unbearable. The curtains were drawn, the light turned out. At last the conference of the Wacholder-Würz Committee, called with a view to voiding Würzian existence, could begin. Leo cleared his throat. Instinctively the conferees reached for their underwear.

Ladies and gentlemen, I shall begin with an introduction. Certain fundamental problems of existence must be clarified before we can deal specifically with the existence of Ossias Würz. First of all, let us consider the question of our own existence. We owe our own human existence to a Polish longhaired sheep from Zakopane. The lamb of God is this very same sheep, and everything that exists is its doing. This sheep is the primal mother of the human race. The human race is one-third Polish, one-third Jewish and the last third German. In every Pole there lurks a Jew, in every Jew a German and in every German a Pole. And conversely, a peg in every hole. (At this point most of the conferees had their trousers on.) This, like everything else, Leo cried out fervently, I call the placental theory of existence, and the six-fingered hand, which at all times holds the Lord's hole open to bring new blessings and new fragrance upon our world, is, I contend, the placental dialectic of materialism. (Here a few who had misunderstood his words cried out: Disgusting.) After this first mutter of dissatisfaction, Leo assumed if possible an even prouder look than before. He raised his voice: The power of these six fingers, ladies and gentlemen, born of the threefold unity, supports the heavenly scrotum and maintains the heavenly cock in permanent erection. The time has come to tell you, ladies and gentlemen, that compared to God's cock, the Cologne cathedral stood on the spire of Saint Stephan's would be no more than the puny pecker of a baby midget, and with the primordial power of millions of workers, my honored friends, that hand tears the manna out of the divine column, tears it out so mightily that it floods the whole earth with a superabundance of consumer goods and full employment, and will forever. *Et maneat semper.* That power of the human six-fingered hand, ladies and gentlemen, is our human existence. It has proved itself by its power. We pull on God's cock, therefore we are. *Penem Dei tractamus ergo sumus.* (The ladies had already put on their brassieres, the gentlemen were reaching for their pocket combs.) As true as I'm standing here! But now let us turn for a moment to the far lesser problem of Würzian existence.

We men and women from every walk of life, encouraged by the kind and generous support of Her Excellency the Minister of Commerce and Reconstruction, Dr. Gertrude Böckling (brief but general applause), have gathered here for the purpose of removing existence from a mortal enemy of our society, a Mr. Ossias Würz, residing at Mel-

chiorstrasse 9, occupation none. Ossias Würz has refused
to leave his hiding place, that den of thieves, although we
have summoned him almost eighty times to do so. He
also refuses to receive any of his friends, and I am referring
most specifically to his oldest friend, Roman Wacholder.
(Wacholder blushed and looked away in embarrassment.)
He has been living on the immoral earnings of his wife's
minor sons because, so he claims, he does not wish to in-
terrupt his progressive labors on his house. These are the
facts we are faced with. In our estimation, honored ladies
and gentlemen, this Würz is a dangerous individual, an
enemy of society, an enemy of freedom, as his voluntary
exclusion and seclusion amply demonstrate. This Würz
can only be destroyed by an action, an action of solidarity.
As of now and for all time, all of us together must ignore
his existence. I request you to raise your hands unanimously, in unanimous expression of our common will,
which I formulate as follows: a Würz does not exist; there
is no Würz. But if one of you, a single one of you should
be of a different opinion, please do not wait for the vote,
the vote must and shall be unanimous.

As usual at this type of congress, where people eat
drink and fuck at someone else's expense, no one wished
to mar the general harmony. All were silent. The silence
lasted two minutes. Long enough to give Leo an impres-
sion of unanimous consent. In that case, ladies and gentlemen . . .

He did not complete the sentence. Mercy, Aslan cried
aloud, I plead for mercy for Würz. He was agitated, he
spoke nervously and repeatedly lost the thread.

It was on a day when death was still common in the city. I still understand nothing. It was hot like today, hot and sultry. A day for sleepers and maters, a day for mothers at the Central Cemetery. Everybody was going. Half-lame old women made out of green hats, and their brothers and brothers-in-law in their Sunday best, and the children all in blue with white gloves. They carried wreaths and flowers to lay on last year's leaves, on the stones with their inscriptions, and a mouthful of questions: Are you sleeping blissfully with God? Is it nice and quiet in eternity? Are you with the Lord now, Mother? There was a sleepy stillness in the street. Like every Sunday, I was waiting for Wacholder. At about three I hear his cane as he comes sniffling down to my room, eleven times he taps it, three times he knocks at the door. He came in. At once I noticed the change in him. I saw it in his yellow eyes, in his thick lips. It's happened, I want to scream, tell me about it. It's happened. But he only gives me a cold, soft hand and catches his breath, the stairs are too much for him, he can't speak. He straightens his collar as if he had come to introduce himself. On his head, in his brown hair I notice something new. A black ship, an enormous hat. I notice a wide coat that he doesn't take off. He sits down on the edge of the bed, holding his coat with his left hand, plants his cane firmly on the floor, swinging the handle back and forth, forward and sideways, up and down. Like a bishop making the sign of the cross. I could feel it, today it's finished, this is the end. The door. What's wrong with the door, he screamed suddenly, what have you done to the door? What does he mean? Nothing, I say, nothing. The door is the way it always is. You've sawed it off, he shouts, you've stuffed it or made it shorter or done something to it. Anyway, it's smaller, you can see that. I still don't understand. No, Wacholder, you've grown, it's that vase on your head, that would make any door smaller. I can't calm him down. No, no, you can't tell me that. Something's wrong. The door's smaller, not I, you've grown out of the door.

What now, Wacholder, what now? What should I do? I want to know.

And I want to know what's wrong here, he said, and he examined every object in the room as if he had never been there before.

Hm, and the windows.

But there's nothing wrong with the windows. The windows were as usual. Insulated against the street with rags and cardboard.

Open them, he shouted, open the windows.

But Wacholder, I said, you know. But he wouldn't give in. I pleaded with him: Please, you've got to understand, the stuff up there, you know, the balls and leaves, the ants, the beatles, the tickets, the chocolate wrappers, nothing must be allowed to fall down. Nothing. No, nothing. Everything must stay up there, I'm taking care of your things. (Since the very first day, we had had a tacit agreement that fear of people was not to be mentioned.)

It's your cellar, Wacholder, I've got to take care of your belongings. Out of gratitude to you.

Gratitude? To me? What for?

For everything, because you let me live here.

Now I was convinced that he had come to take me
away and hand me over to the sausage makers. This was
my last hour. I had every reason to feel grateful. I was well
off here. I had a good life. I'd never had such a good life.
Those were my best years. I looked at him, I begged him
to tell me the truth at last. He stood up, turned his back
to me and said: My dear friend, it's happened, you've been
pardoned. The Gypsies have gone away. With their bears
and their bells and their children and the whole works,
they've gone. Now you are here.

They're gone? Suddenly there was something black, it
came from everywhere at once. Fear. Fear such as I'd
never known. I'm afraid, Wacholder, I screamed, I'm
afraid. The blackness got bigger, it was cotton. I could
hardly hear my own words. Afraid, Wacholder. I don't. I
don't want to go, let me stay here. Let me stay here, here
in your cellar, I don't want to go away.

What happened then I don't know, but suddenly I
was standing outside in a bright light. In space. I had fallen upward in defiance of all the laws of gravitation. I
existed. Suddenly I existed, but not the city. The city had
been slaughtered with sharp knives, it was burned and
filled in, the terraces were blind, the cafés were dead.
Ragged figures were following some music that came from
far off. Whichever way you looked, piles of objects. Picture frames, chairs, mounds of knives and forks, empty
bottles, music stands, birdcages, brushes, keys, keys, millions of key—

That's enough, Leo cried. Enough. Some of the conferees had fallen asleep standing up, the noses of others had drooped.

We want to hear something positive, friend Aslan, something positive. All that happened years ago, nobody's interested. Haven't you got something positive to say? Can't you stick to the point?

Yes, that I can, Leo and honored conferees. Whichever way you look in the city today, you see marble and granite and golden belfries. Decorative additions to the landscape. That is positive. The city has been rebuilt, I'd almost forgotten that. The dragons and poisonous snakes, the scavengers and basilisks have crept away into the underbrush, into holes in the earth. They're camouflaged with mottoes and wreaths, nobody recognizes them, they're protected like unique inventions. They live behind marble and granite, under the golden belfries, lurking in wait for us all, even the stones lurk, the landscape is a trap. But as for the trinity that friend Schön-Waldhaus spoke of, I haven't seen a sign of it. The materialist dialectic of his placenta theory is downright pornography, and besides it's false. God is sexless, an erection is therefore out of the question. God has no hole, because the eternal is conceivable only as one and intact. The trinity of Poles, Jews and Germans is a postwar neurosis. That explodes the six-fingered hand. Still, it's perfectly conceivable that an Indian lurks in every American, a Negro in every Indian, a Chinese in every Negro and a Hindu in every Chinese, and, it goes without saying, conversely. Accordingly, if this hole, and there is no reason to postulate its existence, is indeed held open by a hand rather than a foot, I believe we should be justified in speaking of an eight-fingered hand capable of upholding an erection if there were one. But since there is none, the eight-fingered hand is also pointless. From this it follows quite naturally that this world does not exist because it was never created, or that it can exist only if we let people live. I myself didn't exist until Wacholder said: Now you are here. Being-here is the precondition of all existence, hence also of Ossias Würz's existence.

A general muttering, neither pro nor con. It had long been dinnertime. The conferees had to change, they had this and that to attend to. Telephone calls, correspondence and, most important, baths. They looked at their watches.

Wacholder didn't take his eyes off the conferees for one moment. With a quick wave of the hand, he cut through the smoke of his cigarette as if it had been the preceding speaker's words. Before him lay or sat forty conferees, coughing, looking at their watches, picking their ears.

Leo had knocked himself out, everything was coming along fine, tonight we were going to celebrate, everything looked so lovely, in the dining room the tables were set, everybody has a joke on his lips, at last we're rid of Würz, at last, because in the end the nerve poison had proved harmless. Too much moisture in it, too much water, but this magnificent conference, with all these well-dressed ladies and gentlemen in this posh hotel and Böckling paying for it all, and then that idiot comes along, that Aslan, that jackass, and spoils the whole evening for me and everybody else just for the pleasure of hearing himself talk. That's what happens when you adopt a mentally deranged son, or half adopt him, that's what happens when you take up with people who have no understanding. Call him an author? No, he's not an author, he doesn't belong to our cultural milieu. He's not one of us. Our authors are disciplined. They protest when everyone protests and shut up when no one is protesting. If I'd hit him over the head with the very first lines he wrote, this wouldn't have happened. What am I going to do now? It's embarrassing on account of Böckling too. Must have cost a pile of money, a congress like this, and nothing to show for it.

Then you vote against! Wacholder cried angrily.

Yes, said Aslan, I still have that much cultural freedom.

In that case, you're washed up with me. Anyway, I think we can manage without you. What do you say, Leo?

No, I'm sorry, it can't be done. If a single individual recognizes Würz's existence, our whole plan falls through. Come on, vote in favor. What difference does it make?

Be reasonable! cried a few jumbled voices. There's only one placental theory of existence!

No, Aslan insisted, eager for once to show some strength of character, Würz is there, and therefore he stays there.

But you yourself—Wacholder was beside himself—wrote him those threatening letters.

At your instigation, Father—

Vote in favor—Wacholder raised his fist and had to be held back—or I'll knock you dead.

116

No, I am irrevocably against. I'm not crazy. You're all letting him talk you into this. Not I. Würz is there, and there he stays. If he comes of his own free will, all right. If he doesn't come, that's all right too.

What about me, Wacholder bellowed, I can't close an eye all night. I suffer torments. I'm going out of my mind. That doesn't mean a thing to you, does it? Show that you're grateful, now you have a chance to prove it.

That's no proof, Aslan said coldly, no proof at all. I won't do anything that would impair my own reason. Würz means nothing to me.

I can't understand that, Aslan.

It's simple. If I do something crazy when I know it's crazy, I am seceding from human society. If I didn't know the truth, it would be different. But I do know. Würz is there.

But not if everybody agrees to negate him, that's why we need unanimity.

The whole lot of you can stand on your heads, I know what's true and what's not true. Würz exists and so he's there and that's that. Wacholder and Leo can talk their heads off, as far as I'm concerned—they're crazy windbags. I'm warning you.

Aslan turned quickly and was out the door in an instant. There was nothing for the others to do but throw up their hands and wag their heads.

Soon Leo and Wacholder followed him. The conferees went to dinner as planned.

13 At home on his own bed after the conference, Aslan wished himself in Greenland, where he had already wished Würz and wished all the Wacholders and Würzes in the world, but he couldn't stand it very long in Greenland, because it bored him, and nevertheless he wanted to get away from here, from this city, from this country, from this world, to the Devil, who was no help to him, who as far back as he could remember turned up each year on the sixth of December in the company of Saint Nicholas and chased the children, or to heaven, where he visualized a God who, small, dark and unwashed, showed a strong outward resemblance to Leo, whom he wished the Devil would take, and all that he wished so fervently and with so much devotion that in less than half an hour he was in heaven, after a stroll at the edge of a forest where suddenly Leo had jumped out from behind a tree and cut off his leg with an ax. After this assault his Easter stroll became a calvary, a crawling on both hands and one knee, dragging his left foot in a high shoe behind him by a thin tendon like a crazy cat that somebody has let loose after tying his bloody prey to his tail. In agony he had dragged himself to the secluded hut of an elderly pensioner, a lonely grandfather type who kept turning himself into a grandmother and back, and in all his transformations sounded like Wacholder.

my goodness boy you're still alive who ever made such a mess out of you? just wait the big lummox he'll hear from me when he comes home. not coming? how do you know? he'll come you can bank on that he'll come it may take a while but he'll come he's got to or i'll make mincemeat out of him.

how can you make mincemeat out of him if he doesn't turn up?

naturally if he doesn't turn up i can't make mincemeat out of him but he'll turn up because he's always turned up so far so he'll turn up all right. force of habit and the minute he comes in *bim bam* he'll get one on the dome but you're still looking glum as if i hadn't sworn because what kind of a father would beat up his son out of a clear sky even if he deserved it. no kind eh? right i am. no father would do that to his son because a son is only a child what do you know about fathers and sons you haven't got any son and with a daughter that you haven't got either i almost said even everything is different. you don't hit daughters. you put daughters in a home. between you and me i'd much sooner have had a daughter because with sons i don't have to tell you after all you've told me anyway with sons you get nothing but and this is one more case to prove it with sons you get nothing but heartbreak. sons you've got to beat and daughters you've got to put in a home if you want them to amount to something everybody knows that children never amount to anything and why because fathers nowadays are too soft and soft-hearted. being a father isn't easy i knew a father for instance who spoiled his children and always gave in to them and put up with everything they did and do you know what happened to him you won't believe me but this man haber is his name or i should say was a good fellow and all that but soft really weak this man was the victim of his softness he died of apricot dumplings what has that to do with his character? perfectly simple this haber was always letting people tell him what to do and that's why things turned out the way they did i think it was in july or june '37 or it may have been in august haber comes home from work what he did nobody ever found out it was none of their business either although naturally people spread rumors when somebody makes a secret of his occupation foreign currency everybody thought and probably it was true because rumors not only have long ears they also have a kernel of truth. am i right? anyway this haber hasn't even been home an hour when his wife says don't sleep julius we're going out to eat and he trots along like a lamb. they eat. taste good yes it tastes good. okay and after dinner you're not to lie down but haber wants to lie down after dinner because he always lies down after dinner because he was simply tired a man still has the right to be tired then his daughters chime in i don't remember the girls' names papa they say we want to go swimming will you come along. no says haber i'm not going i'm tired i'm going to lie down for an hour the girls begin to snivel and pester him and say if you won't go we won't go either but we won't let you sleep either we'll holler the whole time here beside your

bed so you won't get a wink so haber thinks it over what
good will it do me to lie down if they won't let me sleep
all right he says i'll go but i won't go in the water i'll go
with you i'll take a blanket and lie down in the grass and
watch you swim so far so good he takes a blanket and they
go to the danube he thinks he'll lie down in the grass as
soon as they're in the water the two of them start sniveling
again father if you won't go in the water we won't either
good says haber then stay here and play in the grass no the
girls scream we don't want to play in the grass we want to
go in the water then go in the water no we won't go in the
water without you because we can't swim i can't swim
either says haber and he's already closing his eyes you've
got to go with us the daughters yell you've got to watch
out so we don't go too far then stay right here i'll watch
out all right nothing doing the monsters yell if you don't
come we'll be afraid and if you don't watch out we might
drown and here in the grass on the blanket you'll drop
right off to sleep and you won't see us no no i won't shut
my eyes i'll watch out aw come on in come in just for ten
minutes but children i have no swimming trunks here
doesn't matter they both yell you always go in in your underdrawers besides haber remembers besides i've eaten
apricot dumplings and people shouldn't go in the water
on a full stomach it's hot the children scream we're dying
of the heat come in come in haber realizes of course that
it's no use trying to sleep with such a racket good he says
i'll go in but only for ten minutes to make a long story
short they go in the water and since it's really hot he
washes himself and dives under and goes into the water

far enough so nobody can see he has underdrawers on he hasn't been in the water ten minutes when he says i feel sick he goes home the children run after him a way then they change their minds and go back to the blanket to play cards meanwhile he's gone home yelling i'm sick they let him lie down a doctor he yells quick a doctor his sister-in-law mrs schor now i remember the children's names too finni and sisi were their names mrs schor runs to get the doctor their regular doctor isn't there he's on vacation or someplace by the time she gets back with the second doctor haber is dead. heart attack. so there's an example for you. and now will you finally tell me what he did to you the thug what happened to your shoe my it's gone that's a fact you've lost one there it is over there in the doorway goodness what's that sticking out it can't be why that's a chunk of foot and the whole floor is full of blood it looks to me like the little rascal chopped your foot off and you don't say a word and i didn't let you talk now i see what he's done goodness that's terrible we'll have to get a doctor right away or two doctors and right away but where can we find a doctor so fast here in the country it takes three hours to find a doctor and we haven't any telephone here lie down lie down this minute let it drip on the newspaper or the floor will get even filthier it's all got to be scrubbed and me a widower i have no wife to do all those things for me my goodness and you're so decent about it and you don't say a thing that scamp that criminal doing that to you i'll show him we need a doctor a doctor this minute you're dying right before my eyes what can i do for you god almighty i'll get you a sip of water there now you're feeling better it'll soon be over pray god for forgiveness for what you've done whatever you've done he'll forgive you the heavenly father forgives everything he'll forgive you for everything whatever you've done.

Will He also forgive me for bashing your Son's head in with the same ax? Will He forgive that too?

To that the old man knew no answer, because he hadn't expected that, and Aslan died. But even in heaven he wasn't shut of the two of them. Leo was sitting there officiating as God, though he was only the Son of God and you could see that the Son, not the Father, was running the shop, as though the Son had sent the Father out into the kitchen garden of Eden, but he, Aslan, had come here to find his better world, to take it back down with him to earth and to Custom House No. 8 and at last to give his title a book, and as a prelude to his festive mood, for a death immediately followed by a better world that can be put between book covers rates a celebration, he was looking for a heavenly festivity or two, such as a resurrection and ascension on the Sunday after the crucifixion, but landed instead in a heaven full of high closed windows lit up by naked low-hanging light bulbs, the deserted study hall of a university closed for midterm vacation. There were a few chairs and tables standing around, on the walls hung the torn-off ends of paper garlands, in the corner a broom beside a small pile of sweepings. God entered through the farthermost door in the ill-fitting suit of a 1927 university professor from Bratislava and snarled a salutation as though it were an impudence to take up the time of so important an official with such stupid expectations of heaven. Why was it so dark here? Aslan asked. That was none of his business, and why this musty provincial smell of dust and old prayer books and Sunday School? That was none of his business either. And why was everybody creeping so shamedfacedly and gloomily through the beautiful old building, as if not only in vacation time but during the school year as well the place were frequented by professors and cleaning women instead of students?

the sun isn't rising today and your private complaints don't interest me, they're no concern of mine, god croaked, and every day isn't easter, the rabbits haven't laid any eggs this year, so we've postponed the resurrection ceremonies from easter to christmas and come again, sir, but don't go yet . . . in the first place, in the second place and moreover. in the first place that incident this afternoon: i felled you with an ax and you got even by bashing my skull in. then you go to my father's, for two hours you don't say a word, you let the old man talk and talk because what counts, mr. what was the name, right aslan, what counts mr. aslan is your own guilt. that will be clear in a moment. in the second place greenland we'll speak of that in the first place. moreover and in the third place we're going to call a spade a spade after that i'll throw you out.

Aslan's first thought was: This fellow isn't very congenial; his second was: The fellow is downright uncongenial; his third was: congenial or uncongenial, pleasant or unpleasant, he would find out the truth. No, this God didn't appeal to him, that was already the truth. This intelligent perhaps but narrow-minded man who loves people like Albert Schweitzer and Martin Buber, the Queen of England and Martin Luther King doesn't love him, Aslan, and that was the truth. Not to mention the autograph hunters, bishops, boy scouts and upright, respectable citizens with whom He no doubt always surrounds Himself. Behind the university-professor disguise lurked the psychotic and degenerate provincialism that talks about respectability honesty hard work and learning and is the bastion of mediocrity.

God, who naturally can read thoughts, had soon guessed Aslan's. Compared to the flow of words that God now turned on him, his brain tincture was mere sugar water: it's not my fault if you don't like me, i love you all the same. you know what i mean. in a purely physical sense. spiritually i don't find you very interesting. greenland proved it. in greenland in the ice you could have given your imagination free rein instead of looking for unfamiliar and dangerous forest trails where somebody would trip you up and chop your foot off you should have stayed in greenland in that abstract landscape i was rather surprised to see you leave so soon what have you got to say to that? nothing. so greenland didn't appeal to you, you'd rather run around with unwashed, lice-ridden people who are kind of mad in addition that's what you like in fact it almost looks to me as if you found the mad people in civilization more interesting than my primitive half-savages that i sent up there so they could wave at you in the form of eskimos when you arrived. you say you're interested in primitives because only primitive people have a kind of madness that something can be learned from, but actually you don't learn a thing once you've taken a look at the neuroses and hallucinations of primitive peoples you think there's hope for civilized man and you beat it. Back to the lice-ridden characters that are still crazy even when they're not lice-ridden. as far as you're concerned everybody is crazy and with those lunatics in the city naturally it's easy to unload your pessimism it's so nice so easy so convenient i don't like that in you i wouldn't have expected you to have anything to do with that kind of people or to have anything to do with civilization in general because a man who doesn't want to help people shouldn't have anything to do with people. no, you ought to be a little more optimistic, it won't take much effort, it will do if you just show a little more understanding for human weaknesses a little more real sympathy that's what they want from you from their fellow-man they're boring i admit very boring to tell the truth if all you do is make them ridiculous and end up by saying people are very wicked and ought to get better in other words if you're a headshaker. why not come right out and say people are evil period and the crummiest of the lot are the austrians but even that is an exaggeration the germans are at least as crummy and the russians americans negroes jews indians and chinese aren't exactly attractive either. no i won't let you get a word in like father like son i have a few more things to say before i throw you out. i don't like it that you didn't look around a little among the eskimos before you came here though i have to admit that it's much more important to settle accounts with the austrians than to love eskimos because there's nothing else to be done with eskimos than love them that's right. eskimos are imaginary people they don't remind us of anything we know here possibly the eskimos used to be cannibals but they haven't been for a long time besides they mostly did it ceremonially or there was a natural catastrophe as in 1892 when one winter followed another without any summer and everything froze up solid. the sea was a thirty-foot wall of ice. they couldn't hunt or fish so first they ate their kayaks then their shoes and finally their women and children. but that's a long time ago and it was a natural catastrophe. i know what you're thinking there hasn't been any natural catastrophe around here except unemployment and poverty and we've had them every-where and always and nevertheless the austrians actually carried out their threats and first beat up the foreigners and then robbed them and then murdered them you've never forgiven them for that there must be a reason not because you're a foreigner you're not all that foreign no peculiarly because you hate foreigners so much you can't forgive them for not calling you in to help with the rob-bing or murdering that's the guilt of your generation. you're sincere though what sense is there in feeling sin-cerely guilty about crimes you didn't commit. that's meta-physical leo. a man's got to look into the future and forget guilt and the guilty and if he can't forget them he's a sentimental nervous nellie which you're proving by not being in greenland but hanging around the lord here like a dog. just leave those people alone. they want to be left alone. don't cry over spilt milk, leave people in peace but if they don't leave you in peace naturally i understand that you've got to defend yourself except i can't see what they're doing to you now they're neither worse nor better than other people and certainly not so dangerous certain things have changed in our country the young people are more enlightened have you noticed they wouldn't do such things nowadays they're too enlightened. i don't say they're fond of foreigners or wouldn't kill the people who were called foreign the cosmopolitan intellectuals. before hitler they were divided the intellectuals persecuted the intellectuals the rich the rich and the poor the poor when hitler came in everybody persecuted everybody at once the poor the rich and the rich the poor. today persecution is infrequent because tomorrow everybody's going to be slaughtered. today you only have a right to say austrian if you mean the whites in the east and west in other words if you think that nothing has really changed and that's what you do think. but that dear aslan is your own fault. you can't unburden yourself here in this world go to the eskimos. either/or.

How was one to address this God? Aslan tried "Herr Doktor," which had always proved adequate in everyday life: herr doktor your sermon has been most edifying and

you have driven me to the crucial question. austria or es-
kimo. that is the question. i am here to gather material
for my novel *the better world* but though miracles were
rare on earth there seem to be none at all up here. i may
have had difficulties with the unreality of life but here
to tell the honest truth the worst kind of nonsense
is dispensed beside which even leo's placental theory
of existence is tasteless sugar water because my moral indignation isn't moral indignation i need guilt for my better world. to feel real indignation you have to live with
both feet in the world to be a socialist for instance which
sounds good because nobody is. i will retire to greenlandic
aesthetics herr doktor as soon as i've thrown off my guilt
and the only way of doing that is to retire in despair to
greenland. our austria is in greenland packed once more in
pack ice. in the smooth ice of art. that is a world apart,
reserved for skaters and the happy savages of literature
who dance gleefully on both legs. it is a pipe dream herr
doktor an alternative that is no alternative. it's a dream
herr doktor like this heaven and no help to us. we'll never
be rid of austria even if we write in greenlandic like some
of my fellow writers. that only makes the problem more
unintelligible. aestheticism won't rid us of guilt. behind
an iceberg of hypersensitivity there's nothing but insensi-
bility. the city is as bad as its people, herr doktor, and we
really can't abolish it. the devices we've devised are nerve
slop and placental lunacy. *the better world*, herr doktor, is
the title of my book. you can't make a better world by
spiriting away the shit that's lying around the country with
high-sounding words. that's regressive herr doktor even if

you give yourself modern progressive airs like leo. the modern savages herr doktor are abysmally provincial. their darkness is as dark as this heaven of yours. i thank you for the audience.

after this excursion aslan was even more determined than before never to finish his book out of sheer stubbornness he resolved to go on turning out manuscript goethes for no other purpose than to make leo's noseo-genetic placental theory blow up in leo's face. and if only the wacholders could be abolished, aslan dreamed, i'd move out, i'd go to greenland i'd be the first to go, but what for? he decided to stay at custom house no. 8 and he wished leo in greenland leo who had provoked him so long with his nonsense that in the end there was nothing left for him but to defend würz whom he had no desire whatever to defend. no he really wasn't interested in würz but only in his own reason and in expressing disloyalty. he was pleased with the cowardice of the conferees and pleased with this excursion, he'd use it for his better world.

14 A better world? Well, at least it's more fun than at home with Father Würz.

Soliciting was fun. It amused the brothers to approach

people sitting defenseless in the bus, cautiously crossing the street, patiently waiting in line for theater tickets, with obscene propositions. It would amuse them as long as the world contained people who were scared to death when they heard such words as screwing, fucking, bucking, or tearing off a piece, especially since the people who had been scared to death were the best customers.

Arnulf and Arnold counted on that and on loneliness. Especially pensioned old gentlemen, dishwashers, waiters and policemen. Not to mention the loneliness of gas men, judges and newspaper vendors. There was no shortage of money in the city. There was more money than patience and as much as loneliness. You can make a living by it, and that was no drawback either, especially since it was also fun. But why no women and girls, Arnulf? Würz had asked once. No objection, Father, but the market isn't so hot. I took one upstairs once. Free of charge. I reached under her sweater. Big tits. Herta was her name. She squirted milk in my eyes. Had narrow gums. She said: I'm stupid. I said: Stupid, stupid, nobody's really stupid. But I am stupid, she said. You should know all the stupid things I've done. I never get anywhere. Because I'm stupid. I have pretty legs. I know that. I don't go with everybody. Only when I feel like it. I played with her all evening, but it was boring. And her gums were too narrow. Doesn't drink, doesn't smoke, only wants to dance. And the Beatles. Old-fashioned. I'm crazy about dancing, she says. Candlelight, good dinner. With those narrow gums. No, girls are no good and there's no percentage. That one wasn't stupid, she was just plain dumb. What good is love if you can't even buy a necktie with it? No, it's no joke. Rita's sons (begotten by a foreign dentist during the war) had decided when they were only twelve and thirteen to stay with Würz and nevertheless to preserve their good humor. Arnulf was tall, much too tall, he had big blue eyes, heavy lids, a weak chin. Much too pretty lips, girl's lips. Long wrists, fingers and toes. A dull look in the eyes, as if they'd been brown—calf's eyes. He jiggled and ambled and wiggled a calf's rear end. The younger was the bull. Even so they looked alike. As much alike as father and son, Würz often thought. The younger has a finer-cut face. Suits him better, Würz thought. His nose is thinner, his chin firmer, his eyes are brown, his hair dark. What expression in those eyes. Doesn't read Cronin and Axel Munthe like his brother, but he's more congenial all the same. The two of them had one thing in common: pop, fashions, clothes, shoes, buckles, bright scarves and small hats. Otherwise they weren't interested in anything. They dress up, they make pop, they want to run the world, and they're always cheerful. And that's that. Water waves, permanents. One combs the other. A world of barbers. Whiskey, chewing gum, finger-tapping. Coca-Cola and records. And pop. And soliciting. Would you like to fuck, sir? I don't do it for fun, believe me, I do it for money (which is not entirely true). My mother pays me even when she wants to masturbate me.

You don't say. Your mother masturbates you?

What of it? I've done the same for her.

What a way for a child to talk. And then your father gave you a good licking, I'll bet.

My father? Why? He said if you do it with her, you can do it with me too. I'm your father, after all. You've jerked off your brother and laid your sister, you've gone to bed with your aunt and fucked your grannie. Now it's my turn.

A fine family. Sounds like Sodom and Gomorrah to me!

I wouldn't say that. We've never done anything with animals except Choo-choo, our dachshund, that sucks us all off for a piece of sugar.

A dachshund!

Yes, a brown one. He was still a puppy.

What happened to him?

We took him to the pound, and they poisoned him. To pay our debts, Mama said. Yes, he had to atone for all of us. Poor fellow.

And now?

Now I don't masturbate at home any more, I'm sore at my family, I still do it in the bus if there's somebody I like sitting next to me. May I go with you?

You're a nice little chap. Do you always speak to people in buses?

Not everybody.

And it always takes?

Almost always.

And how old are you?

Sixteen.

And what's your name?

Arnold Würz. My brother's name is Arnulf. He's sitting over there, that one, see him? The one with the long neck, talking to the man.

Does your brother talk the same way?

No. He's much more vulgar. May I come with you? I haven't much time. I have to get back to work.

Why, what else do you do?

I'm a barber.

And what do you do with all the money you make?

I've got to take it home to my parents. If I don't, my father beats me.

Well, come along.

On the day of the anniversary the brothers came home at five o'clock, shouting the then fashionable battle cry Rockabyebaby, and immediately went upstairs to change.

A mild autumnal piety had come over him at an early hour. The boys were home. The goodies were on the table, and the piety increased: everywhere yellow leaves, brown chestnuts and Sunday afternoon on the lake. And everybody asleep and happy. It's a beautiful day, a swell day, a day with bows and hoops and balloons. A day for playing blindman's buff and climbing trees, for watching elephants and feeding monkeys. God's sun is shining, the world is beautiful, rotating or, if you prefer, walking in radiance. A day for festivities, for nutcracking and apple-peeling, for playing cards and laying out matches, a day for coat-brushing and necktie-tying, for shoe-polishing. A day for a fresh, sweet-smelling handkerchief. As if there had never been such days before, he bounded blissfully about the room like a squirrel (his hands hanging down limp from his chin), jumped with both legs at once and wished for a mustache and long brown hair on his tail. I'm so grateful, he said to himself, grateful to the precious sun, grateful to the blessed sky and grateful because the whole house smells so good. It smells of roast and cake and fresh coffee. He kept stumbling over an empty tin, bottle or pot, and couldn't make out what they were doing in his hallway. Who could have put them there? Rita doesn't do such things. The boys are too old. Strange. Does it mean anything? He opened a few of the boxes. They were empty. Then it doesn't mean anything, Würz said to himself. The void is a pleasure, there's no danger in air. Air is pure, air is clean—did I ever doubt it? From now on, Würz decided, I'll take it easy, everything in due time, if you can't make it today, tomorrow or the day after will do. Where's the fire? Nobody's going to run away with the house. Too bad that I still can't laugh, but there hasn't been time enough, there's been so much to do in the last few days. Anyway, it's not important. Laughing in itself is nothing. If there's nothing to laugh about, that's no tragedy either. All the same, I'm a cheerful man. By nature.

a cheerful man, a happy nature, that was his discovery on this important day. how simple this life is and how much simpler it could be. from now on, würz, let's be on the slow-but-sure side, a sprinkling more of tomorrow than today, and why not?

it wasn't worth the trouble and so on, everything in due time and there's no use driving yourself to and so on, for life passes all too soon and so on—

and off and for that very reason.

man is good, würz chimed at the table, yes indeed. good. and so are we all. good. we dear good people. you dear good world. and so on. with turrets and battlements and drawbridges, castle words. a chiming of easter bells. son of man. child of man. i, you, he, she, it. all human people. god knows, he was a man himself once. everything is good and decent. everything and all of us. even the wicked are good. thanks to motherbirth. not classical god-birth. that was slavery, mass murder. the world is better. the new age is motherbirth. what comes of a mother is good. responsibility, earnestness, freedom. we must band together, form ties. everything good is good. everybody is human. even the wicked are good, as good as the good if not better. everything is good or becoming good. evil is in-human like the good. man is inhuman, therefore he is good. the truth proves the opposite. and so on. therefore happy landings. *prosit.* your health. silence. long silence. nothing but eyes on all sides. eyes from one to the other. jackal, gull, hawk, cat, calf and bull and dog and pig, eyes in the menagerie. rita felt them inside her. the wooden hawk, the glass gull, the whipped dog. don't go on like this, rita dreams into the silence. she feels good. do it all at once, rita prays, don't be ashamed. we know each other. intimate family circle. stab me in the belly, go ahead, even if it hurts. good things hurt. würz became a loving father and husband again. thin milk and pastry dough. i'm innocent and that ought to be enough. i didn't make the city, i'm not god. i'm innocence. no reproaches, please. domestic tyrant? me? certainly not. pedantic perhaps, occasionally, now and then, and a stickler for order, yes, why not? a fault? who is without faults? i admit it's fun, it's a game, it's amusing, it's delightful to live in neatness and order, not like other people, haven't you any sense of humor? man isn't a herd, he's an individual, kindly think of it in that light, my dear fellow workers. esteemed colleagues, peace and harmony and happiness, don't you agree? don't you?

only his sons' and rita's eyes, and their answer to don't you is no.

how are you going to do it? with a dagger? a revolver? a submachine gun. i myself am unarmed, i'm a middleman. all in accordance with custom and the rules of the game. you won't harm me, i know you won't, because i haven't deserved it.

but if you must, please do it right away and i mean now, this minute. throw me down, chloroform mask and then torture, i know. that's the way it's done. first anesthesia to deaden the pain, and then torture, that's how it's done. i know all about it. and then you'll go to work on me. go ahead. i can't wait. i'm dying with impatience. go ahead if that's what you want. now, instantly. you want me to help you, no, rita will help you, won't you, rita, you'll help them, won't you?

no? the eyes were a *won't* and a *no*.

then you won't? and why not, why not? is something wrong? what's wrong? or will you? what do the gentlemen say? nothing? then the session is adjourned, father's going to bed, tomorrow's another day. life and so on. am i right?

two heads wagged as one. a doll's head revolving around its own neck. rita sagged on her chair, all watery, still dripping, as if someone had hung her out to dry.

würz: say something!

arnulf: kna kna and bla bla, i'm dumb.

if you want to dissect me, do it with words. dissectomy würz, würz screamed. i am cleanliness, order, industry, future, purpose, air, pure breathing, decency, take me as i am, but without words there's nothing but barking, nothing but sounds. nothing but sounds. this way. this is the way. he crawled up on the table, knelt down under the lamp between cups and plates, glasses and remnants of food, and barked.

that's the way it's done. to show you that no animal frightens me. don't i bark nicely? he barked again, very loud this time. his barking became a long, drawn-out howling. then he fell still. he lay on the table motionless with open eyes, stiff and stony, and noticed nothing when his sons left with suitcases.

rita sat beside him, held his hand and grieved.

now at last you're still. your mouth is closed. this is the way i like you. powerless.

a silent forest. now you can hear the atoms, now you can feel them. outside the world is dying. the walls are falling, we're sitting in the open. up there are orion and the great bear. it's cold.

würz replied with a buzzing, a long, drawn-out *m* through his nose. now and then he interrupted the *m* to smell his own hands.

15 Whether things were going well he didn't know, but they were going better. It was beginning to look as if Leo's magic had worked even without the congress. No scenes, no letters. In the paper there was giggling and kissing and no more sobbing. He lay sleepy in the appointed place in the mound of paper, a little nest, roughly in the center of the mountain, six feet down, and waited. She still drove out in the official Chevrolet, even though the whole town knew or perhaps because they knew.

Something inside me has turned to pap, daydreamed an overheated Wacholder. How can I feel so indifferent? On account of Trude? And because everything's taken care of now? Did I ever dream I'd be fucking a minister? And as officially as you please. We're practically engaged. Even now I can get anything I want from her. And I don't want anything. All I want is to feel good. I'm gayer than I used to be. Intercourse with diplomats suits me. A woman who smells good, who's rich and has a Ph.D., has always been my cookie. It's made me stupid, but who cares? Can't do me any harm. Happy people always get that way. Thank

God, I've got stupider, that only proves I'm happy. In the old days everything was deadly solemn, hush-hush and flowerpots and Central Cemetery and murder and robbery and arson and rape. But now that I know what I know, if I'd only known before (what he knew wasn't quite clear to him) I'd have been entirely different long ago. Because actually I'm the gay type. Not gloomy. Neither melancholic nor choleric. As mild as an angel and always in a good humor. With two cases of whoopies and one case of hurrahs. The heils unfortunately have run out on me, they were no good. Only gave you sore muscles.

Over there, my dear friend Würz is hopping up and down stairs with his paintbrushes, and I can stretch out here and nobody bothers me.

Upstairs lives our dear good Leo, clever, hard-working and always gay, and right next to him my Benjamin, whom I can be proud of. Because he's shown them how to show character. The way they all started raising their paws again when Leo dished out his absurdities. That's what people are like around here. They haven't changed. What can you do with such a people? All you can do is leave them the way they are. In this country, character isn't a gift from heaven. What isn't brought to them on a silver platter, these people don't want. That's my people, O my beloved country! What a degenerate flea circus you turned out to be. Who are these people, anyway? I don't know them. I don't belong here. Actually, I'm an American. Chicago's my town. There I'm an honest shirt presser and sex murderer in spite of himself. America, that's the country for you. What is this land of roast chicken by comparison? A few mountains, a little water and a little night music. That's my country. The country of men without character. In this country a man's ashamed to have character. A country where Würz is afraid to crawl out of his den because he can't stand the air isn't a country, I wouldn't want to live in such a place. A country where nothing is accomplished with a nerve shower that everybody understands, is that a country? A country that shipped off its own citizens as if they were rabbits for Christmas and has the gall to complain about it now is no country at all. I can't stand it here any more.

He compared this country with abroad and decided that abroad had the advantage of being bigger. Yes, abroad it would be different, Wacholder sighed, oh, if only I were abroad, where every self-respecting citizen speaks a foreign language and respects himself for it, no, I can't stand it here any more, he lamented, I'm dying. He had the Liptauer blues.

here she comes my dear trude and now she came in woman's clothes because everybody knew anyway that the minister was a woman and because wacholder preferred the woman about her to the minister in her. böckling's cunt was based on the thesis: the woman about me and the minister of commerce and reconstruction in me. a perversion no doubt, *sans doubte*, said böckling when as was seldom the case she conversed with wacholder. wacholder loved her, if only because she could speak foreign languages. she was always saying words like *benissimo, grazie,* or *merci* and *bon, bon.* for him, she was an out-and-out foreigner, a little conceited perhaps, a little high and mighty but she had her good points. he was happy, no he was proud that a lady like her of the highest society had so cordially adopted him and his blind brother. by order of the minister of the government so to speak wacholder had to play all day with his brother as a grandfather with his grandchild so as to hand him to grandma in the evening in guise of grandchild. for all i care you can be a father to my brother in that case i'm your cock's aunt but i won't let him treat you as a son because then your cock would be my uncle. i can do without that, thank you. she couldn't have made it clearer than in these plain official terms that the purpose of her visits was honorable. no bestial fucking between government and people but a decent family relationship between old party members. no sooner was trude settled in the nest than wacholder pursued the purpose. of this purpose he knew a dozen variations: o lovely lovely purpose, o dear sweet purpose, o great big purpose, o best beloved purpose, o ultimate purpose, o front purpose, side purpose, hind purpose. this patriotic work song was followed by his own private words of admiration. the menu of a widely traveled man who knew a thing or two about the good things of this life. more ardently and louder than usual he whispered his favorite love words and failed to hear the newspaperman who had crept into the hay unnoticed after böckling. he wanted his scoop. the reporter dictated into his microphone, wacholder's words of love punctuated his remarks:

Here I am in the hay that looks like paper, feels like
oh you, my darling kirsch
paper but can't be paper because
    prune whip, hungarian goulash
it isn't. The mound is a hundred feet
pork chops, pork sausage, golden Wiener schnitzel
wide, thirty-feet-high caverns, hiding places,
    belly paths
my pear brandy, my omelet, my fresh
you can only get around on your belly here
cucumber salad, o my liver dumpling
which is just what a nude male functionary of sub-
you soufflé, you pig's foot
section D is doing on top of a lady of the highest
society. He is copulating with her—whispering
with horse radish and mustard.
    The closeness of their embrace precludes noncopulation.
It can't be a headwaiter advertising his menu. I have
crept to the edge of the crater, I am now on the highest
peak of the volcano and in a position
    just another drop of that 1947 brandy and one
      more
    to observe the copulation in every detail. The
      state is being
    cup of coffee and another helping of whipped
      cream
    gutted before my very eyes. She has
    and hand over the Liptauer, pass the Swiss
      cheese,

allowed herself to be governed horizontally in-
where's the Camembert and where's the soup
stead of the other way around. When low-grade
    functionaries are permitted to worm their way into
    authority from above
Where's the stuffed egg
something must be done.
Pass me the cake.
And without delay. I could make a horn out
    of paper
yes all mixed up, that's the way I like it,
I could make two. And the mask
where's my salami and here so soon comes the salad
of a ferocious beast could also be made from paper
with holes for eyes and mouth with a few deft
strokes of the pen, very well, I'll do it.
You're roasted calves' brains with fried
    potatoes
and I'll transform myself into the German
    bull, the Teutonic steer
where are the applesauce and the raspberry
    cake,
now I'm a bull descending the face of the
    mountain,
ah, there it is. It's all here, all finished.
and I roar a loud loud moo. It worked. The clerk
has jumped up. Another moo, that's for you, customs
clerk, and another boo for your shameful deed. He's embarrassed, he modestly rolls his duster in a sheet of paper.

Instead of pulling it in, he's ashamed and wraps it up. He has recognized me as a bull. The old lion retreats before the young lion. The illustrious lady raises her head, sighs My goodness and falls back on her paper pillow. She too has recognized me. As a reporter for the *Neueste Nachrichten.*

Disguise is pointless now. I see, Your Excellency, something I would rather not have seen. The Fatherland dishonored by intimacy with a common man of the lowest classes. I have no opinion, I am a newspaperman, but my readers will now be able to form one. I have seen through you. And the gentleman over there who is looking at me with such horror has seen through me. I am not only the *Neueste Nachrichten,* I am also the Teutonic bull. More than reporting, fucking is my specialty, I might say my passion. He has seen the light. He knows. He has wisely wrapped his inferior birdie, that I wouldn't even wish on my ten-year-old daughter, in paper. It's trash, Your Excellency.

Cowering perplexed in a corner of the nest, he clung to the vanishing remains of his brother and decided something must be wrong. Either he's not a man or he's not a bull. He's not mythological and he's not funny either. He's spoiled my fun at the best moment. Who is it? Or is it a what? If he were a man, we'd have heard him. If he were a bull, he wouldn't pester me. He must be both.

The newspaperman dictated into his microphone: Her excellency the minister is now dressing. now she's putting on her corset, now her stockings, i don't want to see any more, i can't see any more, that's enough. what have you to say to our readers, frau doktor?

böckling sat down, half dressed as she was, in the lap of the press, and announced: i have always, on and off duty, stood up for the interests of my government and my people. it is not enough to sermon the strayed sheep of the shepherd from braunau on the inn, and it is not in the best interest of our country to punish them all their lives because they once made mistakes. it is indispensable that the last remnant of the nation, and this customs clerk is the last of the last, should find their way back into the bosom of the community. his prompt resignation came as a disappointment to me.

what have you to say to that, mr. wacholder, speak into the microphone, please.

moo, wacholder moaned, i don't want to talk now, i want to think.

he leaned back to think and thought: this is really the first time. what do you say to that, brother? it never bothered us before, we shared everything, and not just with one bull but with eighty million oxen. this fellow's not from the newspaper, he's lying. he really is an ox, a brutal opportunist, and he thinks he can scare an old fighter like me. what's this? where are you, brother? he unwrapped the roll of paper. the package was empty.

he dressed and left the warm nest by an emergency exit. looking back, he saw his trude, his own trude, in the arms of the reporter, who was hugging her with his paper tail.

aslan and leo were asleep, and for the first time wacholder didn't dare to wake them. i'm not an animal, he whispered into the void, not i. no, i'm not an animal, but i'm not anything else either.

two days later between the house wall and the elderberry bush back and forth the main thing was to avoid all verticals sharp stones sticks and his own shadow. avoid verticals and if possible prohibit them the horizontal was vertical too. abolish roads and rivers, abolish pipes, no, i'm not a pipe and not a hose that was long ago and thank god not a salt stick, children would bite him off and beer drinkers. he didn't want to be a roll either or own one. if bread then a loaf and aslan should write round books or i'll take him apart and put him in the drawer and leo should think rounder thoughts or i'll have to fold him up and put him in the sideboard. then there'd be no further obstacle to roundness. he himself round and inconspicuous a milk-wagon wheel würz doesn't shoot at milk wagons, he'd roll into melchiorstrasse and if that's still too big a coin würz would have no answer to that because money is blond and aryan and beautiful. only it didn't help him any because he had no money and was therefore worthless. a rag-and-bottle man, old rags, old bottles. i buy everything, only nothing pointed, i've got principles, because my feet were kind of long too, i counted to thirty a round number. always been a secret counter (if only i'd counted the paper on time) he counted to three: one two three and opened his eyes, he'd done it even as a child and every day he counted his few belongings in a little chest done it even as a child an old habit, even counted the length of a yawn which wasn't easy and now he counted his own breaths and that was new and it was new too that in spite of all the verticals and all the counting the day was bright as if nothing concerned him. hadn't aslan wished him a good day? and you could rely on aslan. if he said good day it was a good day (you couldn't count on leo in this connection, if leo said good day a storm came up) but aslan had said good day and there it was. his birthday. zero day. that was long ago and now everything's the same. old bottles and rags, wacholder cried . . . and looked up. at the window stood leo. his hands, both hands outstretched. what are you doing, leo?

an experiment, you see my hands coming out the window at the end of my extended arms, my body didn't stretch them out, on the contrary my hands put my body into the room and there it stands. man is a T. i've proved it. the T is true existence. that is the geometry of existence, it's not placental. posture, wacholder. it's how you lie. not where.

no verticals, leo, please no verticals.

you've got to lie lengthwise, wacholder, but this time completely.

his was longer, leo.

but no longer than a wacholder lying full length, old man, do it.

you want me to take the horizontal, leo? i can't.

make yourself as long as you can and you can.

i can't, leo.

lie down, wacholder! get into geometry. no nonsense about that, wacholder, it's the surest position.

geometry is all verticals, leo, at least for me.

lie down, wacholder. maybe you'll get to know round circles too and the other figures.

wacholder lay down between the house wall and the elderberry bush.

is this all right, leo? am i long enough?

you're on the right track, wacholder. make a round hole.

wacholder drew a hole with his finger. is it round enough leo?

now it's going to be harder, wacholder, now you've got to try to climb into the round by yourself, the first thing is to dig a decent hole that you'll fit into.

wacholder ran for a shovel, came back and began digging. is this right, leo?

a little deeper, wacholder, but you're doing all right. wacholder stood up to his waist in the freshly dug grave. am i deep enough, leo? it strikes me as funny.

just go on like that, wacholder, you'll be in a perfect circle before you know it.

is that geometry, leo?

it's your only chance.

am i deep enough, leo?

pretty near, wacholder, just go on digging.

i can't leo, i can't go deeper or i won't get out again.

then take a handful of earth, wacholder, and start filling in. good, wacholder, very good.

leo, i'm burying myself.

it's high time, wacholder.

where's aslan, leo?

father, where am i? where are you, wacholder?
here, aslan, down here, don't you see me?
don't go any deeper, father, come back. you're burying
yourself.
aslan, watch out, i see a vulture.
it's your birdie, wacholder.
don't crack jokes now, leo, i'm almost dead.
father, you're almost dead.
i know, aslan, any birdie's my vulture.
your vulture is an eagle. a double eagle.
it's a stinker, leo.
then die like a man.
father, i've got to laugh.
aslan, i'm not a joke.
who says you're not, wacholder?
an eagle with two heads is no joke, leo, it's no topic of
conversation.
i've already laughed, father.
all right, aslan, go right on laughing in the meantime
i'll die.

and he died just to give the others something to laugh
about, but the others didn't laugh.

ABOUT THE AUTHOR

Jakov Lind, born in Vienna in 1927, was eleven years old when the Germans occupied Austria. He escaped to Holland, and later spent two years in Germany, using forged identity papers. After a series of jobs—among them construction worker, fisherman, photographer and orange picker—Lind settled in England, where he now lives with his wife and two children. His highly acclaimed volume of stories, *Soul of Wood,* has been translated into fourteen languages. His novel *Landscape in Concrete* furthered his reputation as one of the finest postwar writers.